Remembering

Michael Colin Macpherson

Green Duck Press
MT Shasta, California

Remembering

Green Duck Press
Post Office Box 651
MT Shasta, CA 96067

Cover Art, "Lemuria," Kay Ekwall, MT Shasta, CA 96067

ISBN No. 0-9642136-0-5

Library of Congress Catalog Card Number: 94-96488

Printed in the United States of America
10 9 8 7 6 5 4 3 2 1

For the Family of Light, and especially for my teachers and my companions along the way, Saint Germain and Alarius.

Contents

1 A Gentle Touching of the Heart 1
2 Brothers and Sisters 7
3 Shining City 16
4 Remembering 25
5 Secrets 31
6 Doorway to the Heart 38
7 Dreaming the Same Dream 47
8 The King Must Die 54
9 The Weather Changes 60
10 Quake! 68
11 The Quake is Felt in Mount Shasta 75
12 The Aftermath 81
13 The King Needs Gold 88
14 Susan's Revelation 95
15 The Mark of the Beast 103
16 More About the Beast 109
17 Friends Gather Together 117
18 Truth 124
19 The Cashless Society 132
20 Broken Promises, Shattered Dreams 140
21 Life at the Sunshine Cafe 146
22 Power Centers 152
23 Mount Shasta Says No! 159
24 The Gathering 164
25 Susan Speaks Out 169
26 Repercussions 176
27 Susan is Tested 184
28 Friends Gather Again 191
29 Community 201

Acknowledgments

My thanks to all the people who read my manuscript and offered encouragement and advice. My special thanks to Mary Baker for her thoughtful comments; to Kay Ekwall for her beautiful painting which became the front cover of *Remembering*; and to Yola Kaskey and my wife Mary Ann for their caring and meticulous proofreading. And to Spirit…Always.

Chapter One
A Gentle Touching of the Heart

Revelations: 1:19: Write the things which thou hast seen, and the things which are, and the things which shall be hereafter.

February, 1997

Susan Langley woke slowly to the chirping of birds outside the window of her Mill Valley, California, home. She yawned and stretched, careful not to wake her husband Jeff; but he was already awake.

"You getting up?" Jeff asked sleepily.

"I'm going to make us some breakfast," Susan answered.

"Hey, it's Sunday. You don't have to get up yet."

Susan didn't respond. She slipped on her faded blue robe and padded into the bathroom. Her Golden Retriever, Sam, lifted his head and watched her go.

Examining herself in the mirror, she had the strangest sensation that the green eyes staring back at her belonged to someone else—but of course that was impossible. She switched on the light, leaned closer, and gazed deeply into her own eyes. For a moment, something seemed to flicker there, something that she had never seen before. She shook her head. No, she must be imagining things—people's eyes don't change overnight. She sighed. She brushed her teeth, washed her face, gave her short black hair a few quick brush strokes, then walked back through the bedroom on her way to the kitchen. Jeff watched from under the covers. "Why not come back to bed for awhile?" he suggested lovingly.

Susan shook her head no. Most mornings she would have joyfully accepted his invitation, but this morning she felt preoccupied.

She'd had one of her odd dreams—her "Seth" dreams Jeff called them. They weren't exactly nightmares, but they *were* a bit disturbing. She began having them about a month ago after reading one of the "Seth" books channeled by Jane Roberts.

"Why not read one?" she had suggested to Jeff. She loved the books and wanted very much for him to love them too.

"No way," he'd replied. "Sorry, but this channeling business makes no sense to me. Besides, I think the books and those channeling sessions you're attending are scaring you. They aren't good for you."

Susan disagreed. She loved the books *and* the sessions.

In the kitchen, she got the coffee from the refrigerator and the filters from the cupboard. She turned on the stove to heat the water. Sam sat on the floor, his liquid brown eyes gazing up at her expectantly, his bushy tail thumping on the linoleum.

"I'll feed you in a minute, Sam."

She sat at the table. Closing her eyes, she willed herself back into the dream. She relaxed and opened to that mysterious other dimension. She *welcomed* it.

She was floating down a languid green river on a rubber raft, the hot sun overhead. She was alone. She floated into a narrow gorge. High up on a cliff, overlooking the river, she saw her mother and father and her sister Ellen waving their arms frantically. They were yelling at her, but the sound of the river drowned out their voices. Suddenly, the water began slapping the sides of the raft. She was in the rapids and there was nothing she could do except hold on and pray she wouldn't tip over. The rough water tossed the raft around as if it was a toy. Her arms ached from the effort of gripping the slippery rubber. She couldn't last much longer! But just as she was about to give up, she skidded around a bend into calm water. There was even a little beach where she might rest. She relaxed her grip, only to be thrown to the side of the raft as it slammed into a submerged rock. The raft tipped precariously. She was going to capsize!

Then she woke up.

How did the dream end? She peered inside only to have the dream evaporate in the effort of trying to remember.

The shrill whistle of the teakettle pulled her back into the present moment. She poured a little water into the paper filter, waited a moment, then poured in the remaining water. She breathed in the comforting aroma of the rich, dark coffee.

Sam's wet nose nuzzled her leg. "Sorry, sweetie, I forgot about you."

She fed Sam, sat back down and closed her eyes. What did it mean, being on a raft? She asked for help in understanding the dream. A journey! Of course, that's what the raft represented. Now, what about the water? Was water sexual? She wasn't sure. But the rapids and the rock, those were surely signs of danger. A dangerous journey! Was she about to embark on a dangerous journey? She opened her eyes and sat for a moment pondering exactly what that might mean.

In the corner, Sam sat hunched over his bowl, happily and noisily crunching his breakfast.

Still preoccupied with the meaning of the dream, Susan went outside into the bright winter sunshine and retrieved the Sunday *San Francisco Ledger*. Back inside, she heard the sounds of Jeff's shower. She opened the paper, stopping at the travel section. The picture of Mount Shasta leaped out at her! The Mountain hypnotized her. She scanned the story beneath the picture—a typical *Ledger* story, half serious, half tongue in cheek. The writer told of an ancient race of beings called Lemurians who, some claimed, lived inside the Mountain. Of course the writer didn't believe in Lemurians himself, that much was clear from the story, although he hinted that many people who lived around the Mountain *did* believe in such fairy tales. New Age kooks he implied, without actually saying so. Susan thought living inside a mountain seemed quite possible, even quite intriguing. Did that make *her* a New Age kook?

From the bedroom came the sounds of Jeff's off-key singing. He was preparing for his Sunday morning bike ride up Mount Tam...alone, for she did not share his love of cycling.

"Hi hon," Jeff greeted her cheerily.

"Mm."

He poured himself a cup of coffee, turned around, and leaned his 6-foot frame against the counter. "You seem deep in thought this morning."

"Uh-huh."

"Did you have another of your dreams?"

He could be very intuitive when he allowed it, she thought. "Yes, I did."

Putting his coffee down, he walked over and hugged her. "I love you, you know. It's just that I don't *understand* you sometimes."

"You don't understand *yourself*," she replied, hoping she didn't sound judgmental, but knowing she probably did.

His first impulse was to deny what she had said, but she was right. Even his friend and racquetball partner, Glenn, had commented on his general state of confusion. "Maybe it's a mid-life crisis," Glenn had joked. Jeff doubted it. After all, he was only thirty-eight. But he did have to admit that *something* was happening.

With a pained expression on her face, Susan said, "I'm sorry. I..."

"It's fine."

"No, it's not. I don't think it's you at all. I think it's *me* I don't understand."

Jeff wrinkled his nose at her. "It's both of us."

"Okay."

Neither knew what to say after that. Sam rescued them from the uncomfortable silence by scratching on the kitchen door.

"Why not take him with you," Susan suggested. "He needs the exercise."

"Sure. You want to go?" Jeff asked Sam.

Sam barked and clawed frantically at the door.

"Okay, let's get you ready." Jeff reached inside the kitchen drawer for Sam's red bandanna and tied it around Sam's ample neck. "Now you're all set, big guy."

"Jeff, don't you think it's extremely warm today?"

"It's probably one of those false springs we get every year at this time."

Susan shook her head. "It's more than that. I can feel it. It's almost like it's late spring or early summer. It doesn't feel like February at all."

Jeff had recently begun paying more attention to these "feelings" of hers. She often knew things even when there was no logical way she could. "Now that you mention it, it *does* feel warm. What does the paper say?"

Susan turned to the weather page. "It's supposed to be about 55 today, but it's lots warmer than that...and it's only 9 in the morning."

Jeff finished tying Sam's bandanna. He glanced out the window at the big deck thermometer. "Holy cow, it says 75. Hey, that can't be right. It must be broken."

Susan shook her head. "I don't think so. I think the weather is changing. I know that sounds weird, but I can *feel* it."

"Changing? You mean like *permanently* changing?"

"Maybe. And something else. Doesn't it feel like things are moving faster now?"

"Like what things?" Jeff asked, mystified.

"Like...*everything*. Like our *lives*."

"Oh, *that*." Now he felt on familiar ground. "Well, that's what you get for living in California. Everything moves quicker here. Life in the fast lane you know."

Susan was impatient with his joking. "No, I don't mean

that. I mean it's almost as if we're in a different time zone."

"Well…"

"It's the oddest feeling. Like I'm standing still and everything else is speeding up around me. Or maybe it's the other way around. The people at the channeling were talking about it. They said the vibrations are faster now, and the funny thing is, I knew exactly what they were talking about. Only I can't quite put it into words." She banged her fist softly on the table. "I *want* to, but I can't find the words."

"Look, I don't know about vibrations. All I know is, my body says it's time to have a cup of coffee and pedal up the mountain."

She hadn't heard a word he'd said. "Jeff, let's go to Mount Shasta for a few days. Remember, we almost stopped there once on our way back from Oregon."

"Sure. We'll talk about it. I gotta go."

Susan heard Jeff unlock his bicycle. She heard the heavy metal chain clank onto the concrete floor. She heard Sam bark excitedly. She stared outside the window, feeling unfocused, almost as if she was dreaming. She shivered. Was someone else in the room? Looking around, she saw no one. Yet the feeling persisted, and she was momentarily afraid. She let go of her fear and immediately felt arms— unseen, loving arms—enfolding her. In that moment, Susan felt very protected and very much at peace with herself.

Chapter Two
Brothers and Sisters

Revelations: 3:17: Because thou sayest, I am rich, and increased with goods, and have need of nothing; and knowest not that thou art wretched, and miserable, and poor, and blind, and naked.

Susan was right. It *was* warm—extraordinarily warm. CALIFORNIA BAKES UNDER WINTER HEAT WAVE! The headlines screamed.

The day after Susan's dream the temperature soared to an unbearable 97 degrees in the San Francisco Bay Area, far above anything ever recorded for that time of year. That same day, the little town of Truckee, nestled high in the Sierra Nevada Mountains on Interstate 80, recorded an 85, an almost unheard of temperature even for the middle of summer—and it was only February.

By the fifth day of the heat wave, the Sierra snow pack, which usually stayed intact until May or June, began melting at a furious rate, sending torrents of icy mountain water cascading down steep Sierra slopes, swelling the creeks and rivers of the lowlands, causing serious winter flooding.

It was extraordinarily warm. It was *abnormally* warm, and this worried even the usually laid back Californians.

Although Susan was an avid newspaper reader, she quit

reading about the heat wave. She objected to the tone of the stories. They didn't take it seriously, treating it as some passing freak of nature and nothing to be concerned about. Susan didn't agree.

The papers *did* have some interesting tidbits of news, though, *if* you knew where to find them.

Susan had long ago decided that newspapers hid the best news stories in the back pages of the paper; and that is where she found an item that piqued her interest. It seemed that several small to midsized banks had failed in the past few weeks. Most were in the Midwest, but two were in California. The Tipton administration, the story reported, had no comment, and the Chairman of the Federal Reserve denied that the country was in for a series of banking failures similar to the disastrous and expensive Savings and Loan failures that had taken place a few years before: "The banking system in this country is sound," he assured the public. "A few failures here and there are to be expected in today's diversified economy and are absolutely no cause for concern," he had added. Susan had seen this man on television several times. He reminded her of a used car salesman—a *sleazy* used car salesman. She didn't trust him, so the story and the Chairman's denials troubled her. She searched the papers for the next three days hoping for some more news; but, like so many other interesting stories she attempted to follow, it mysteriously vanished. Susan felt frustrated at being denied access to what, in her opinion, was important information.

The heat wave dragged into its second week. There was a run on fans at Jeff's hardware store. He seriously considered ordering a few air conditioners, but waited, hoping, like many Californians, that the abnormally hot weather would soon end.

The strange weather was even beginning to fool Mother Nature. Many trees, confused by the sudden, abrupt shift in temperature into believing that spring had arrived, sent out their fragrant blossoms months ahead of schedule. And hordes of chipmunks and squirrels, lured from their winter nesting places by the hot sun, chittered their pleasure at the warm weather.

Many of the human inhabitants of the state were not so happy, however. The novelty of the unusual weather had worn off. Tempers were short and nerves frayed. Law enforcement agencies around the state reported dramatic increases in violent crime, and mental health workers struggled to cope with an avalanche of calls from those upset by the abnormal weather.

It was the wrong time of the year for a heat wave.

Susan and Jeff decided to flee the muggy Bay Area and head for the relative coolness of Mount Shasta. They invited Jeff's friend, Glenn, and his wife, Vicki, to accompany them.

"I knew we should have gotten air-conditioning in this thing," Jeff joked as they drove through the blazing heat of the Sacramento Valley. Even with the windows down, it was still oppressively hot in the car.

They passed a roadside sign advertising the Apple Orchard, a popular restaurant and gift shop on Highway 80.

"Let's stop for lunch," Vicki suggested.

Jeff pulled into the large, sprawling parking lot surrounding the Apple Orchard and parked under the shade of a huge walnut tree.

Glenn pointed to the flashing blue lights of what appeared to be a police car. "Looks like trouble," he said.

Coming abreast of the patrol car, they found four of the Apple Orchard's security officers surrounding an old and battered white station wagon. Through the grimy, dirt-encrusted windows of the car, they glimpsed a woman and three children.

Jeff approached the officers and asked, "So, what's the problem?"

One of the security officers, a tall, beefy man about twenty-four, sweat staining the underarms of his olive green uniform, whirled around and scowled. "Nothing we can't handle, sir. Now we'd appreciate it if you'd move along and let us do our job!" he barked.

Susan craned her neck to see into the station wagon. The woman, in her early twenties, stared straight ahead, her thin hands clutching the steering wheel. Two older blond girls—Susan guessed they were the woman's daughters—crouched in the back seat amid cardboard boxes stuffed with clothes and an assortment of cooking utensils. A younger girl, perhaps three or four years old, her eyes huge with fright, sat huddled in the front seat next to her mother.

Jeff held up his hands. "Didn't mean to bother you. Just curious."

The officer relaxed. "These people have been living here in their car for three or four days. We can't allow it. You can understand that, huh?"

Susan peered into the front seat, gazed into the child's frightened eyes, and smiled; but the child, her face frozen in fear, looked right through her.

Vicki turned to the security officer, the concern obvious on her face. "Maybe they need help. Maybe one of them is sick."

The security officer placed his hands on his hips. "That's not our problem, ma'am. This here is private property, not no campground. They gotta go."

Susan wanted to say something. She wanted to stand up for this woman, to let her know someone was on her side, but the words stuck in her throat. When she asked herself why, she knew it was because she was *afraid*.

The security officer took a step towards Jeff. "Now if you'd move along, we'll take care of this," he growled.

Jeff shrugged his shoulders. "Okay, gang, nothing we can do here. Let's go."

As Susan walked away, she felt the hot flush of shame for not speaking up. She consoled herself with the thought that there must be a good reason for her paralyzing fear, but it didn't help dispel her guilt.

As the sliding glass doors of the Apple Orchard whooshed closed behind them, they were immediately swallowed up by throngs of shoppers crowding around tables piled high with exotic and sometimes expensive merchandise. After the heat of the parking lot, the air conditioned atmosphere felt chilly.

Susan stifled an urge to glance back outside to see what was happening with the station wagon and its inhabitants. She tried to interest herself in the bustling scene before her, but the soft Latin music from the overhead speakers and the almost cloying aroma of freshly baked goods coming from somewhere in the store began to nauseate her. She grabbed Jeff's arm to steady herself.

"You okay, hon?" Jeff asked.

"Fine," Susan answered, feeling uncomfortable with the lie.

"I felt bad for those guys back there," Jeff remarked, as if picking up Susan's feelings.

Glenn shook his head sadly. "It's like that everywhere these days. When was the last time you were in a big city? Seems like half the people are homeless. It's really grim. Those folks back there are lucky to have a car to live in."

Susan shot Glenn an angry glance. "You really think so?"

"Well, I didn't mean..." Glenn stammered.

"I know. Sorry, Glenn," Susan replied, not wanting to take her anger out on her friend.

Feeling uncomfortable with the way the conversation was going, Jeff intervened. "Boy, it sure doesn't seem like the recession has hit *this* place," he said as the four of them threaded their way through the crowd of frantic shoppers.

Surveying the scene before him, Glenn said, "Just because people spend money doesn't mean they can really afford it. These folks are maxed out. Most of them are spending money they don't have to forget how much in debt they are. It's an addiction—like getting drunk to drown your sorrows."

A Wall Street broker for many years, the pressures of "The Street" and the stresses of trying to survive in New York City had worn Glenn down. So, after a painful bout with ulcers and a scary trip to the emergency room with chest pains, he and Vicki decided to shed the tension of the big city. They moved to a quiet country home in Marin

County where Glenn now taught two classes in economics at Marin University and where he spent most of the rest of his time puttering in his garden. He still had many friends back on Wall Street, though, and he loved to talk about his experiences; and he loved to expound on the state of the economy—as *he* saw it.

Glenn lingered at one of the tables and picked up a pair of jade dolphins, rubbing his hands lovingly over the deep green stone. "Nice," he murmured. Giving the carving to Vicki, he asked, "Can we afford this?"

She turned it over and examined the price tag. "Sure, if you want to hire yourself out to cut all the lawns in the neighborhood for a couple of months." She glanced again at the price. "Make it three months," she added, handing the dolphins back to Glenn.

"It might almost be worth it. Say, by the way, how much do I get for cutting *our* lawn? We never discussed that."

"Sorry, buddy, it comes with the territory."

Reluctantly, Glenn returned the carving to the table. "Anyway, as I was saying." He scratched his head. "What *was* I talking about?"

Vicki laughed. "The economy, what else?"

"Oh yes. Well, the way I see it, it's bad news the way everyone is going into debt. Especially here in California. I'll tell you something else—lots of the players on the Street are getting nervous over this. These are pretty cool customers. It takes a lot to get them nervous, but nervous they are. Scared is more like it."

They arrived at the entrance to the indoor restaurant, gave their names to the hostess, then sat down on blue corduroy-upholstered benches to wait.

Jeff asked, "If everyone is worried about the debt, why don't they do something about it?"

Glenn needed no further prompting. "Well first of all, it's difficult to understand what's going on in the economy. Numbers wise I mean. You can't get any straight answers out of Washington. They lie. They lie about everything. So everyone's guessing."

Although Susan already knew the government's penchant for lying, still, Glenn's vehement tone surprised her. "Do people in *Washington* know the government is lying?"

"Oh, sure," Glenn answered casually.

"What do they lie about?" Jeff asked.

Glenn threw up his hands in dramatic fashion. "Everything! For instance, take unemployment. What does the government say it is? 11 percent? No way. It's more like 25 percent."

"You mean it's 25 percent in the inner cities," Jeff corrected him.

"Nope, it's more like 40 or 50 percent in those places. No, I'm talking about *here*, in California, the *whole* of California. Got it? 25 percent. So, how does Washington get away with saying it's 11 percent? Simple, they only count the people they want to count." Glenn hesitated. When he was sure that he had everyone's attention, he continued, "Take the poor slob who's beaten his brains out searching for work. His benefits run out, right? So he gives up and moves in with the in-laws. He's unemployed, right? At least you and *I* would say so; but, because he's not actively looking for work, they don't count him anymore. It's a lie. If you asked the Washington numbers-crunchers about it, they'd have some reasonable sounding explanation, reasonable sounding unless you stopped and thought about it. Then it would sound like horseshit. Which it is. Washington has more horseshit per square foot than any other place I've ever seen. I guess that's how they grow all those beautiful cherry trees."

A green clad hostess arrived and led them to a thickly carpeted room. Wall murals depicted scenes from the early history of California. In the center of the room stood a huge, multisided glass aviary teeming with dozens of gaily colored tropical birds.

They sat down and Glenn continued, "It's funny, but I think President Tipton is beginning to understand the truth about Washington, about the lies and all. And in spite of all the horseshit he has to deal with, some of his programs are pretty far out—enlightened economics in my opinion. But they're just jerking him around. They let him talk all he wants—and Lord knows the man *does* like to talk—and they let him take his bus trips. Then, when he's done, they pat him on the back and call him the "peoples" President." Glenn sighed. "Then the power brokers go right on making their slimy deals. Personally, I think we're in deep trouble, guys."

Jeff glanced at Glenn quizzically. "Like?"

Glenn didn't respond right away. He moved his silver-ware around absentmindedly. "Like the whole damn system coming apart."

"Oh, come on, you've been saying that for years, sweetie," Vicki chided.

Glenn regarded her for a long moment. "I suppose. But…this is different. I can *feel* it."

Their food arrived. The waitress placed Susan's beautifully sculpted garden salad in front of her. Susan speared a slice of perfectly ripe avocado, took a nibble, then put down her fork. She fought to control the tears welling up in her eyes. She got up from the table hurriedly, almost tipping over the vase of fresh flowers. "I'll be back in a minute," she said.

"Hey, hon, anything wrong?" Jeff asked, the worry obvious in his voice.

"No, I'm fine. I'm fine. I'll be right back." Susan pushed her way through the tangle of shoppers, bumping into a man in a tan sports coat. "Sorry!" she called over her shoulder. Outside, the blast of hot valley air took her breath away. Walking quickly, she reached the spot where the woman and the three girls had been, but they were gone. She searched up and down the rows of parked cars, but the battered white station wagon and its four occupants had disappeared. The only sign that they had been there was an empty box of cookies and a child's discarded toy lying on the ground. Picking up the toy, she discovered it was a tiny white unicorn with a missing leg. She slipped it into her pocket. She took a deep breath. Sweat trickled down the side of her face. She put her hand into her pocket, clutched the plastic unicorn, and whispered, "I wish you well on your journey little sisters. Perhaps we'll meet again. I hope so." Then she walked slowly back to the restaurant.

Chapter Three
Shining City

Revelations: 21:23: And the city had no need of the sun, neither of the moon, to shine in it: for the glory of God did lighten it, and the Lamb is the light thereof.

The air in the little mountain town of Mount Shasta was cool and refreshing compared to the scorching heat of the upper Sacramento Valley through which they had just traveled.

Mount Shasta was everywhere. Rising to an elevation of over 14,000 ft, it seemed to come right into the town itself.

The Mountain entranced Susan. She could not take her eyes off its snow-covered peaks, and she knew in that moment that some mysterious force had called her here and that she was home.

Home. Home. Home. She repeated the word silently inside herself. What did it mean, anyway? Was it a *place*? Susan didn't think so. Yet in this sparkling little town, perched on the side of this beautiful Mountain, in *this* place she felt the feeling of home; and her heart opened to receive the beautiful understanding.

Jeff squeezed Susan's hand. "Hey, you look happy."

Vicki glanced at Susan and said, "Radiant is the word *I'd* use."

Susan smiled. "I *am* happy. Isn't that the most beautiful Mountain you've ever seen? It's so loving. I never thought a mountain could be loving, but *this* one is."

Glenn had done some research on the Mountain in the past few days. "It was a sacred spot for the Indians around here. Maybe that's what you're picking up."

Deep within her heart, Susan felt the sacredness of the place. Something else, too, something very personal—a resonance, as if she and the Mountain sang the same song. Could mountains really sing? This one could, she decided. Could the others hear the music? She hoped so.

Jeff glanced around at the nearly deserted streets. "I wonder what people here do for a living?"

"It's a ski resort in the winter," Vicki answered. "Lots of our friends come here."

They strolled down the tree-lined main street, pausing occasionally to peer in shop windows. Jeff happily dragged them into the hardware store so he could "check out the local competition" as he put it. Farther down the block, a small blue and white Victorian house caught Susan's attention. Set off the main street, under the shade of three huge and fragrant pine trees, it seemed very different from the other shops and stores they had passed. The simple hand lettered sign in the front window read: SHAMBHALLA; A METAPHYSICAL BOOKSTORE.

Susan tugged on Jeff's arm and said, "I want to go in there."

Jeff nodded. "Sure."

Glenn took Vicki's hand. "Look, guys, I think we'll go on walking. We'll meet you back at the motel."

Susan's intuition told her that Vicki wanted to join them in the bookstore, but she kept this understanding to herself.

The store was cool and dark inside and smelled faintly of flowers. Roses? And something else. Incense?

At first, Susan thought the store was deserted. She was

about to suggest they leave when she spotted a tiny, gray-haired woman, dressed in a forest green jumpsuit, kneeling down arranging books on one of the bottom shelves. On hearing them come in, the woman looked up, and Susan gazed into a pair of the most intense blue eyes she had ever seen. The blue eyes were set in a deeply tanned and wrinkled face. The tiny woman was at least eighty.

The green-clad woman smiled, magically transforming her face into that of a fifteen year old girl. "May I help you?" she asked.

Susan liked her immediately.

"I think we'll browse for awhile," Susan answered, re-turning the woman's smile.

The woman resumed her book straightening. "Sure. Give me a holler if you need help," she called over her shoulder.

Although Susan gave the titles a cursory glance, she realized she was more interested in the elf-like woman and her unusual energy than in the books. Not wanting to ap-pear obvious, she slowly maneuvered herself to where the green-clad woman was working; but she had the strangest feeling that her careful maneuvering was in vain and that the woman was waiting for her.

Feeling nervous for some reason she could not under-stand, Susan said, "Hi. I'm Susan and this is my husband, Jeff."

The woman smiled again, and again the transformation amazed Susan. Did the woman's face truly change or was the light playing tricks? She blinked hard. No, it was no trick, the woman's face *did* change. The lines and wrinkles were still there...or *were* they? Susan couldn't tell.

"Hello Susan and Jeff. I'm Evelyn." Evelyn's voice was so low Susan had to lean forward to hear.

Susan felt awkward, as if she was five years old. "Jeff and I are visiting."

Evelyn raised her eyebrows. "Oh, is that so?" she asked, as if she didn't believe what Susan had just said.

"Well...sure...we're visiting," Susan stammered.

The two women stared at each other.

Feeling uncomfortable, Jeff broke the spell by asking, "Have you lived here long, Evelyn?"

Evelyn didn't answer right away. She glanced out the window at the Mountain. Then she replied softly, "Twenty-two years. Twenty-two years this summer."

Susan felt "spacey." Maybe it was the rarefied mountain air or maybe it was the smell of the flowers or of the incense in the shop, but, whatever it was, she felt very unfocused. This feeling had always intrigued her, had always seemed like an interesting doorway she might someday explore. The problem was, a part of her usually became concerned when she slipped into this altered state. Was this part of her perhaps afraid that she would never return to "reality"? Feeling a twinge of fear now, she tried to clear her mind and focus her thoughts, but it was no use, so she gave in to the "spacey" feeling, went through the doorway, and asked what she needed to ask, "Evelyn, why do people come to this town?"

Evelyn's blue eyes twinkled mischievously. "This town? People don't *come* to this town, not people like you anyway. People like you are usually pulled here. Sometimes they're *dragged* here...by the Mountain. Know what I mean?"

"Yes. How did *you* know?"

Evelyn ignored her question. "They are pulled here to find something."

"I don't know what I'm looking for," Susan blurted out.

Evelyn shrugged her shoulders. "That's okay, you're like the rest of us who were pulled up here. Pretty soon you'll begin to figure out that you don't actually know much, and that most of your *intellectual* understanding is almost worthless...and *very* boring. Then, little by little, you'll quit pretending you have any answers. After that, you'll learn to ask the right questions... and *then* you'll meet exactly the right people—the ones you're *supposed* to meet. Know about them?"

Susan looked deep into Evelyn's eyes. Her brain felt fuzzy and her head throbbed. "The right people? Like you?"

Evelyn shrugged again. "Mm, could be. Matter of fact, I'm having a little gathering at my house tonight. Nothing formal—a few local people. You'll like them. And Veda has promised to channel for us. Veda's a local woman. Her name used to be Carolyn, but she changed it when she started channeling. I can't quite get used to it. I still want to call her Carolyn. Anyway, she channels Saint Germain. Want to come?"

"Sure. Maybe I'll even get Jeff to come," she said. She laughed, remembering his attitude toward channeling.

He surprised her. "Love to," he replied.

Evelyn beamed. "Good. Seven at my house. I'll give you directions."

"Dorothy, do you have any..." Susan began. She clapped her hand over her mouth. "I mean *Evelyn*," she corrected herself, shaking her head. "Now why did I call you Dorothy? *You* didn't change your name, did you?"

"Nope."

"That's weird. I don't know why I said that. Well, anyway, what I wanted to know is, do you have any books on Lemuria?"

Evelyn spun around and was half way down the aisle before Susan caught up with her. "Got a whole row back here. Anything in particular you want to know?"

"I'm not sure. It feels like there's something I need to *understand*. Or to *remember*. But...I don't know what it is."

Evelyn smiled as if she understood perfectly; then she showed Susan the books on Lemuria.

Susan selected a book—a beautiful, old, leather-bound volume called: *Mylokos of Lemuria*. She paid for it, then asked Evelyn, "Evelyn, I hope you don't take this the wrong way, but I have the strangest feeling I've met you before, but...I don't think I have. I mean, I've never been to Mount Shasta, so it's not very likely."

Evelyn slipped Susan's book into a paper bag. "Better get used to it; happens all the time in Mount Shasta. Nothing to worry about. Probably a past life we had together. Now that you mention it, *you* look familiar too."

Evelyn pursed her lips. "It's a past life. Yes…definitely a past life…and it's in Lemuria. See you at 7!" she called out as she vanished behind a row of books.

Susan and Jeff walked down the long brick path leading to the street.

Jeff chuckled. "She's a character."

"Did you like her?"

"Yeah, I did. She's like…what *is* it about her? I've never seen a nature spirit, but I imagine if I did it would look like Evelyn. Know what I mean?"

"Sure, I liked her, too."

Jeff gazed up at Mount Shasta. The late afternoon sun shining off the snow at the summit crowned the Mountain with a pink aura. "You're right about the Mountain—there *is* something special about it. I can feel it."

Susan smiled and took his arm and they walked back to the motel.

Vicki and Glenn agreed to join them at the channeling. "Not that I believe in this kooky stuff mind you," Glenn had protested. "But certain people have unfairly implied that the only things I'm interested in are the Dow Jones Averages and the price of pork belly futures. Absolutely untrue. I have an open mind—a cosmically open mind."

"Whatever you say, pal," Vicki had teased him.

They got to Evelyn's house—an old redwood A frame with a beautiful view of Mount Shasta—promptly at 7. Much to their surprise, they discovered that none of the others had yet arrived.

"Did we get the time wrong?" Susan asked Evelyn.

Evelyn laughed. "No, you're right on time. The others will be along shortly. They'll straggle in about 7:30 I suspect. Hardly anybody's on time here. It's what we call Mount Shasta time. There's Mount Shasta time, and there's the time the rest of the world runs by. You're still running by city time. I expect you'll get used to it."

Evelyn served them her homemade blackberry tea while they waited.

The first to come was a thin, bespectacled man named Brian. Nice, but painfully shy Susan thought. After being introduced to them, Brian took a seat in the far corner, closed his eyes, and disappeared into himself.

Anna, who arrived a moment later, was the exact opposite. Large and boisterous, her energy filled the room. She asked them questions, then paid attention to their replies. This is an unusual place, Susan thought—people actually *listen* to what you have to say.

After Anna had chatted with each of them, she busied herself rearranging furniture.

Next came Cassandra and her friend Emil. They have the same Earth energy that Evelyn has, Susan thought.

Evelyn took Cassandra's hand in her own. "Cassandra is an artist, and Emil...well, Emil does nothing, just lazes around enjoying himself. An aging hippie," Evelyn teased.

Emil had a pained expression on his face, although Susan thought it was mostly a game he played with Evelyn. "Not true. I am writing a book. It is good. You will see," he said. His German accent was obvious.

"It really is good," Cassandra added shyly, clearly proud of him.

Susan wanted to hear more. "What is your book about?" she asked.

"It is about the sacred places of the Earth, places like Delphi and Machu Pichu."

"And the Mountain?"

"Yes, but of course...the Mountain, too. Most certainly."

Then, before Susan could ask any more questions, a frail looking, dark-haired young woman slipped in quietly through the front door. She walked around the edge of the room almost as if she did not want anyone to notice her. They soon spotted her, however, and almost everyone in the room pounced on her and hugged her. They really love her, Susan thought. She wondered what it would feel like to be loved that much.

Evelyn was the last to embrace the young woman. Then she introduced her. "Folks, this is Veda. And Veda, these are our visitors from Marin County: This is Vicki and her husband, Glenn. And Jeff. And this is Susan."

Susan took Veda's hand. Their eyes met. The love in Veda's eyes awed Susan; but there was turmoil there also. Veda was obviously someone who had traveled to the depths of her being and had returned with much wisdom and much understanding. She has been through her own private hell, Susan thought. Yet much seemed unresolved in this woman's life.

"Are you enjoying our little town?" Veda asked the four of them.

Vicki answered for all of them. "It's beautiful. And so quiet."

Veda nodded. "Good. I am glad you are enjoying it. Sometimes people are not so comfortable here."

Veda's remark sounded strangely ominous to Susan — almost like a warning.

"I'm glad to have met you," Veda said. "Now you must excuse me. I must get ready." She took the seat in the middle of the room, the one Susan guessed was reserved for her. Unpacking a small bag, she began setting up the recording equipment she had brought with her, relieved to have something to do.

As Veda readied herself, two more couples arrived. Susan watched as they greeted friends and then found places to sit. Glancing around the room, Susan knew deep within her heart that she was among *friends*. It did not matter that she had just met most of these people. They were lovingly familiar to her. They were *family* — the kind of family she had always wanted and had always known she would someday find.

Evelyn sat down next to Susan. "You must not misunderstand Veda's manner," she said softly so as not to be overheard.

Evelyn's remark caught Susan completely off guard. "Oh, I didn't..."

Evelyn squeezed Susan's arm. "No, no, I was watching. You were put off by her manner."

"A little."

"Veda can appear aloof. It's because the channeling takes so much out of her. It's difficult for her. It *drains* her. It will be easier later, but for now it's difficult. It's something we accept about her. She is much different when she isn't channeling. Not so *serious.*"

"Sure, that makes sense. Thanks, Evelyn."

Veda had finished hooking up her recording equipment. Glancing at Evelyn, she asked, "Everyone here?"

Evelyn twisted around in her chair and faced the group. "Has anyone heard from Carol? Is she coming?"

"No, but she said to say "Hi" to everyone!" someone called out.

Evelyn turned back to Veda. "Okay, then I guess that's it. You all hooked up?"

"I think so," Veda answered, pinning a small microphone onto her white sweater. "How's the volume? Can everyone hear me?"

"Fine!" Anna boomed from the back of the room.

Folding her hands in her lap, Veda said, "Great. I guess we're ready then. I think Saint Germain is coming through tonight…and maybe El Morya. They're talking about it now." She laughed—a shy laugh. "Let's begin by closing our eyes in meditation. This will prepare the way for the Masters to speak through me."

Chapter Four
Remembering

Revelations: 1:1: The revelation of Jesus
Christ, which God gave unto Him, to
show unto his servants things which
shortly must come to pass; and he sent
and signified it by his angel unto his ser-
vant John.

Veda sat up straight, folded her hands in her lap, and
closed her eyes. Others in the room followed her example.
Before Susan did so, she glanced at Vicki. She's afraid, Susan thought. Suddenly aware of her *own* anxiety, she
smiled at Vicki and closed her eyes.

After three or four minutes, Veda began to breath more
deeply. Then she opened her eyes.

Susan was struck by the change in Veda's appearance:
Veda's eyes had darkened, and they now shown forth with
an intensity that had not been there before. Susan shivered.
Those dark and mysterious eyes spoke of hidden worlds
and distant galaxies.

Composed and relaxed now, Veda slowly swung her
gaze around the room, missing nothing. When she spoke, it
was with a different voice, lower and more powerful than
her normal speaking voice: "Greetings, beloved ones. I am
Saint Germain, come this evening to be with you for a

time, to bring you information, if you wish, and to find out
how you are all doing." Saint Germain smiled as he spoke
and his dark eyes flashed.

One person coughed, but except for this the room was
silent for almost a full minute.

"Well, how *are* you doing?" Saint Germain inquired.
His voice was curiously lighthearted, and it was loving.

"Fine," someone murmured. "Quite well," another
whispered.

"Good," Saint Germain responded, obviously pleased.
"And what shall we speak of this evening? What is in your
minds and in your hearts? Questions concerning the coming Earth changes? For they *are* coming you know."

Anna raised her hand. "Yes, would you speak of those."

"All right. What is it you wish to know?"

"Well, there's lots of talk about an earthquake that's
supposed to happen. Some people say it's going to happen
here in California. Is it...I mean, well, what do *you* see?"

Saint Germain paused for a moment as if collecting his
thoughts. "Indeed, beloved one, we may speak of this if
you wish." He paused again. "Of course, that of which you
speak is a possibility. You in California live on the leading
edge, and you love to live dangerously." Someone in the
audience giggled. "But remember," Saint Germain continued, "The quaking of the earth is but a way for your
Mother Earth to heal Herself. It need not be a cause for fear
or concern...unless of course you *really* want to live dangerously, for remember, you always create that which you
fear."

Anxious laughter greeted this remark, followed by
much nervous fidgeting and shifting around by those in the
audience.

After people had quieted down, Saint Germain resumed, "We cannot at this time tell you with certainty that
such an event will occur, or where, although the probabili-
ties at this time are that...Mm...let us say there are pressures
that will probably precipitate this event within this your
next year; and it will be of such a scope that few have
seen." Then, as if reading the high level of anxiety and fear

in the audience, he added, "Remember, beloved ones, this is dependent on many other factors and is therefore a statement of probability only."

There was absolute silence in the room.

Susan's voice shook despite her efforts to control it. "May I ask a question?"

"Of course, beloved one."

"This earthquake...I understand what you mean when you say it's necessary for the Earth to heal Herself, but..."

"It is *one* way," Saint Germain corrected her.

"What do you mean?"

"It is but one way for Mother Earth to heal Herself. There are other ways as well."

"Oh, sure, I understand; but if it happens, will it affect those of us in the Bay Area?"

Again, Saint Germain paused before replying. "This event, if it occurs, will affect all who live in this place you call California—also many who live outside the boundaries of this your state."

"Thanks. You answered my question."

"One moment. I have more to say to you...if you wish."

"To me?"

"Indeed."

"Well, sure."

"You are a wondrous entity you know." Saint Germain gazed deep into Susan's eyes, a mysterious smile on his face. "Do you know how wondrous you are?"

"I guess I do...sometimes."

"Yes, well you are. You understand much. You have been a seer in another lifetime. A *see—er*. Did you know this?"

Susan felt almost hypnotized by the words coming from Veda's mouth. She felt as if Saint Germain had taken her by the hand and was leading her deep within herself. And *yes*, it *was* true, she *had* been a seer in another lifetime—a lifetime as a priestess. She knew this without being able to explain *how* she knew it. It was as if Saint Germain was helping her open some long forgotten memory banks.

Susan drew in a deep breath. "You're right. I was."

"Indeed, and you will be again if you desire. It is up to you."

Susan hesitated before replying. An emotion was sweeping through her. She waited until she could identify it. "I'm not sure about that. I'd like to, but...but I think I'm afraid." Her mouth was dry, her voice quivered, and suddenly salty tears filled her eyes. "I'm afraid," she repeated and looked up to find Saint Germain's dark and penetrating eyes watching her intently.

"Indeed, beloved one," Saint Germain said softly. "And do you understand why?"

"No." Then, almost as if she had flipped a switch, Susan's gaze turned inward and her speech slowed as she began viewing that long ago lifetime as a priestess. "I can see myself. I'm hurt...they hurt me...the people hurt me. They got angry at me and they hurt me," she sobbed. Hot tears slid down her face and fell on her hands folded in her lap.

She felt Jeff's arm around her shoulder. She appreciated that; but she didn't need his support just then—she needed to *remember*. She *wanted* to remember. She shrugged and he took his arm away.

The room was quiet. Someone handed her a box of tissues. She took one and blew her nose.

"Indeed, they *were* angry with you. Do you remember why?"

Susan shook her head no.

"Take yourself back again to that lifetime."

Susan slipped deeper inside herself. It was like diving under water. She saw a crowd of angry people surrounding her...and the terror on her own face as she struggled to escape. "I see a man. He's wearing white robes. He's...I think he's speaking for the rest of them."

"And what is he saying?"

Susan furrowed her brow with the effort of remembering. "He's shouting that I did something...but what could I have done to make them so angry?"

Saint Germain paused for what seemed like an eternity before responding. "You told them something they did not

wish to hear. Something that threatened them greatly. You
told them the *truth*."

"Yes."

"It was very courageous of you."

Susan sighed deeply. "But they wanted to *kill* me. I
think they did kill me. What could I have told them?"

"I will leave that for you to discover on your own,"
Saint Germain replied cryptically.

"Okay. I *will*. I want to understand. I want to *remember*."

"Indeed, the discovery of the truth is very important to
you now, is it not?"

"Yes."

"Yet this has not always been so."

"What do you mean?"

"You have spent many lifetimes hiding the truth from
yourself, have you not?"

Susan felt confused. "What truth?"

"The truth of *you*, beloved one."

Susan considered Saint Germain's words. What did he
mean the "truth" of her? "All I know is, I want to understand who I am and why I am here," she declared clearly
and firmly.

"Indeed, and is this not your truth?"

"I guess so." Then she nodded to herself as if some
awareness had just come to her. "Well, yes, of course it is."

"And is this not what you have been hiding from yourself all these many years?"

"You mean I haven't wanted to know who I am or why
I'm here?"

"Precisely."

"Is that what you mean by hiding the truth of who I
am?"

"Indeed, beloved one."

Suddenly the truth of Saint Germain's words, spoken so
wisely and so lovingly, and given so freely, exploded
within her in a burst of beautiful white light. Yes, she *was*
afraid to be herself, especially to speak the truth of what
she knew. She was afraid others would not like her or that

they would hurt her. This cloud of fear had darkened her whole life. Even as a child it had been so.

She remembered, as a child, being able to see the spirit guides around other people. She clearly saw the guides surrounding her mother and her father. Her parents' guides were beautiful, and she loved them and talked with them as she did her own guides. Why were her parents so unaware of them? With the openhearted innocence of the loving child, she assumed her parents would want to know about these celestial beings...so she told them what she saw. They did not believe her at first. Then they did and it triggered their fear. They told her it was wrong to know such things and dangerous to tell others what she saw. Barely five, she made a choice: She decided that her parents' love and acceptance was more important to her than speaking the truth of what she knew...even if it meant giving up her own beloved guides. So, she willed herself to stop seeing and to stop knowing—she willed herself to *forget*.

Susan cried. She cried for the little girl with love in her heart who only wanted to help. She cried for the child who only wanted to share with others the world she found so loving and so beautiful. She cried for a long time, until there were no more tears; then a wonderful calmness flooded her being.

Chapter Five
Secrets

From *Endtimes,* a privately published book that began to circulate in 1998: "The Forces of Light and the Forces of Darkness were locked in grand combat. Who would win? The winner would be the side that controlled the flow of information."

Through her tears, Susan met Saint Germain's gaze, and the magnetic power of his eyes brought her back to the now moment.

Susan dabbed at her eyes with the tissue. "I don't want to lie anymore. I want to be free to speak my truth."

"And you will be, beloved one."

"How?"

"What is it you fear?"

Susan didn't hesitate. "Speaking the truth and then being hurt because my words threatened someone."

"Indeed; and what is it *precisely* that you fear?"

"Precisely? I'm not sure."

"You fear you will recreate that long ago lifetime when you *were* hurt for speaking your truth."

Susan took a deep breath and let it out slowly. "Mm. So

I'm afraid that I'll upset people and they'll kill me...I mean in *this* lifetime."

"Indeed. That fear is yet within you, and it is such that it paralyzes you. If you wish to heal this fear, you must remember that lifetime, and you must ask for understanding. Ask to understand what you did and why. Then, take the understanding deep within your heart and align the fear. I will help you if you desire this."

"Yes."

"Then it is done. Remember, you live in a very different time now. You may freely express the truth in your heart without fear of reprisal. Not so in times gone by. In those times, you often met a quick and painful death for speaking your truth." He paused and smiled at Susan. "It is not so today, for in these times much freedom is yours...if you desire this. Do you understand?"

"Yes." Suddenly, Susan felt much love for the entity who was speaking through this frail-looking young woman. She knew Saint Germain was her friend and that he loved her as perhaps no one on Earth ever had. "Yes, I understand...at least I am beginning to understand...and I am grateful."

"As am I for having had this opportunity to speak with you. And we will speak again. You have only to call on me you know."

Susan felt loved and she felt reassured. "Thank you."

"Are we finished, beloved one?"

"Yes we're finished. Until next time."

"Indeed, beloved one." Saint Germain's glance lingered for a moment on Susan's face; then he gazed out over the audience, surveying the room with his probing eyes. "Who has a question?"

"I do," Jeff was quick to respond.

"All right."

"What can you tell us about this unusually warm weather we've been having? I've been thinking about it a lot, and it feels like...well...it's odd to say the least."

Saint Germain was quick to reply, "It is not Mother Earth's doing."

It took Jeff a moment to fully comprehend the significance of Saint Germain's remark. "You mean someone—some human being—is actually *doing* it? Making it hotter?"

"Precisely."

Jeff shook his head and laughed nervously. "That's hard to believe. It doesn't seem possible. Who has the technology? Is it really possible to do such a thing?"

"Of course," Saint Germain answered calmly.

"Who would do it? And why?"

"There are those in your government—in your *secret* government—whose intent it is to create fear and confusion in this your population."

"Okay. Let's say someone wants to frighten us. Why choose the weather? I mean it isn't exactly *scary*. It's just *hot* for this time of year."

"This present abnormality is, let us say, a test run to determine if the equipment functions properly—*and* to gauge your reaction."

"You mean there might be more to come?"

"Indeed."

"Why? You say it's to create...how did you put it?"

"It is done by those who wish to create fear and confusion in the population," Saint Germain repeated with loving patience.

"Right. To create fear and confusion. But I still don't see why."

Saint Germain turned the question around. "Why do *you* think, beloved one?"

"I'm not sure."

Emil raised his hand. "May I speak?"

Saint Germain smiled. "Of course."

"I am from Germany, and although I am too young to remember World War Two, my parents told me much about it. They told me how the Nazis devoted much energy to the creation of fear among the people, because they knew that frightened people *obey*."

Saint Germain nodded. "Precisely. And that is the plan at this time—to make human beings in this county more manageable—to make them *obey*. To bring this about, those who would control you have decided to create a deep fear within you. There have been many previous attempts to frighten you into submission, but you are a resilient people, and you do not frighten easily. So those who would control you had to devise new methods to instill this fear. These weather changes are but one of these new methods."

"But why choose the weather?" someone asked Saint Germain.

"The weather impacts you greatly, does it not? Yet most of you take it for granted. You assume that the winter brings the rain and the summer the sun, and that the seasons follow each other with beautiful regularity, as they have always done. You trust Mother Earth to be predictable. So if there is a reversal of patterns, as is happening now, you begin to wonder and then perhaps to worry and by then you are in fear.

"It would be wise of you to understand your fears surrounding such events...and then to dissolve your fears, for those in your secret government have other scenarios planned. What would be your reaction, for instance, if suddenly there were tornadoes in California or earthquakes in Kansas or monsoon rains in your Southwest desert? Many of you would react with panic, or at least with deep foreboding, would you not, for it would appear as if Mother Nature had turned against you. Remember, when your hearts are filled with fear and with panic, you are more easily manipulated."

It was Glenn's turn to ask a question. "After these people, whoever they are, had created these changed patterns, then what?"

"Then those who had created the changes would bring forth solutions. They would seem like saviors, would they not, and they would greatly enhance their authority by this maneuver. Many of your brothers and sisters would then follow them. Many would willingly give their power away and would submit to their control. It has happened many times on your Earth, this giving away of power to those who appear to be all knowing and strong."

Cassandra had been following Saint Germain's remarks with great interest. Now she asked, "What about the earthquake you say may happen? Will that also be created by human beings?"

"No, that is different, that is Mother Nature speaking. However, there are those upon your Planet who have the means to artificially produce such quakings of the Earth. Are you in the understanding of this?"

"No," several voices murmured.

"There is much about your technology you are not in the understanding of, much you have not yet figured out, and much your trusted scientific community withholds from you. Begin to ask questions, beloved ones. Take nothing for granted in these coming days—for truly, nothing is as it seems. Remember how the magician works: He entices you to look away from the hand that performs the trick, does he not? Much that is happening on this your planet has the same purpose—to distract you from seeing the truth. Do not be fooled by such sleight of hand…even if it is performed by those whose authority you would have trusted in the past."

Many others had questions for Saint Germain. He patiently answered each of them. Susan listened for awhile; then she slipped within herself and mulled over what Saint Germain had helped her to understand. Yes, she had an extraordinary ability to know things. And like it or not, this ability—this gift of sight—was again surfacing in her life. She had abandoned this gift as a child because she felt she *had* to. She now promised herself that *she would never again disown this or any other of her gifts*. It was too painful, like cutting away a part of her physical body.

Yet much fear still churned within her. "Please, please, whoever is helping me, please assist me in understanding my fear. Help me to receive the message my fear has for me, and then help me to release my fear." In that moment of deep asking, she knew that someone had heard her and would help.

She also knew she would soon be tested.

Glancing at her watch, she saw it was nearly 9:30. Saint Germain had been speaking for more than two hours.

Saint Germain surveyed the audience. "Are there more questions?" he asked.

Except for some restless stirrings, there was no response from those assembled.

"All right, then, I will take my leave for now. It has been my pleasure to have been with you this evening. But before I leave, let me remind you of something. It is a truth—a great truth—I would remind you of." Saint Germain paused and his dark and mysterious eyes narrowed. "The truth—*your* truth—is that you are powerful entities, and you need not fear what is coming." Saint Germain paused again, looking around the room, focusing briefly and intently on each person. "Understand who you are, beloved ones. Understand that you have come here upon this planet at this time in your history to participate with your Mother in Her healing. It is your choice... *and* it is your opportunity to know your strength and to once again be sovereign. I am with you always, beloved ones. Good evening."

Veda took two deep breaths and slowly opened her eyes. "Thanks for coming," she said simply.

Susan sat down next to Vicki and Glenn. "What did you think?" she asked.

Vicki clapped her hands together. "Wonderful... but kinda spooky. He looks right into you. I mean *right* in. Made me nervous. I was afraid he was going to ask me something. But you did great, Suze."

Susan didn't agree.

Glenn raised his eyebrows and asked Vicki, "What were you afraid of? Some deep, dark secret? Something you've never told me?"

Although Glenn sounded as if he was teasing, the edge in his voice told Susan to look deeper. He's afraid of something, she thought. Only he won't admit it, and he wants to put it off on Vicki, like it's *her* problem.

Vicki shook her head. "No, nothing like that. No deep, dark secrets. It was something else." Glancing shyly at

Susan, she asked, "Suze, do you suppose it's possible I've had a lifetime like yours? Like the one you just saw?"

"I bet you did. If so, maybe Veda and Saint Germain could help you understand it."

While Susan talked with Vicki, Jeff had retrieved their coats. "Ready to go?" he asked Susan.

Jeff's abruptness startled her. "Oh, sure, I guess we can do that," she replied, although the truth was she wanted to stay and visit with her newfound friends.

"Going already?" Evelyn called from across the room.

"Yes!" Susan called back. "I'll drop in at your store tomorrow if you're going to be there!"

"I'll be there!"

Susan was in a dark mood as she walked across the street to their car. Why was Jeff always in such a hurry to leave? Why couldn't he be a bit more social? Why did he always have to be the first one out the door at events like these? She had an impulse to go back inside and let Jeff do what he wanted. But she didn't. She got into the car and pulled on the door. It clicked softly closed.

Chapter Six
Doorway to the Heart

Revelations: 3: 8: I know thy works: behold, I have set before thee an open door,
and no man can shut it: for thou hast a
little strength, and hast kept my word,
and hast not denied my name.

===========

They ate at a colorful local cafe Evelyn recommended.
Susan was silent throughout dinner.

Jeff had been sneaking furtive looks at her the past few
minutes. "You upset with me?" he asked finally.

"No," Susan replied, not yet ready to admit her feelings. She glanced absentmindedly at the paintings by local
artists adorning the walls of the restaurant. Then she looked
across the table at Jeff, her eyes flashing with anger. "Only
I don't see why you wouldn't stay at Evelyn's for awhile."

Jeff appeared surprised. "I didn't think you wanted to."

"Yes you did," Susan snapped back. "And you
wouldn't extend yourself—even for a few minutes. I would
have for *you*."

"I'm sorry. If I'd known..."

"But you *did*. Admit it, you were being selfish and anti-
social."

They deliberately looked away from each other and did
not speak.

Across the room, at a table next to the wall, two couples, obviously enjoying a good joke, laughed uproariously.
Their raucous laughter sounded extraordinarily loud to Susan.

Jeff sighed—a long sigh. "You want to go back?"

"No," Susan replied petulantly. Hearing the tone in her
voice, she knew she was deliberately picking a fight with
her husband. She wanted to understand why. She felt a
gentle prompting to connect with Jeff. "Jeff?"

Jeff didn't look up from his plate.

Was the whole room watching her? It felt like it. "Jeff,
I'm sorry." Then she shook her head, looking disgusted
with herself. "No, wait, that's not what I mean. Let me start
again." She took a deep breath and looked Jeff directly in
the eyes. "I'm in a rotten mood and I'm taking it out on
you." Having said this, a weight lifted from her. "I don't
understand why I'm so grumpy. I guess...I guess I'm irritated with myself for leaving when I didn't want to. So the
truth is, I'm blaming you for something that's not your
fault."

Jeff nodded. "Okay," he mumbled, the hurt still in his
voice.

Susan wanted to say more, to find the words that would
remove his hurt, but she wisely refrained, knowing it was
his own lesson.

Jeff took her hand. "I understand. Thanks," he said
warmly, as if choosing to use the space she had so lovingly
left open for him.

Glenn glanced back and forth between Susan and Jeff
as if he was a spectator at a tennis match. His face assumed
a demeanor of mock seriousness. "Have we figured this out
now? Is it all settled? Are we all healed?"

Susan wanted to strangle him. His sarcastic remarks
often triggered this response in her. She liked Glenn, but
his sense of humor often seemed peculiar—it always came
at the "wrong" time and it always felt a bit hostile. Now,
however, sitting across the table from him, reading his energy, she understood how uncomfortable he was with the
emotional openness she and Jeff had just shared; and she

saw how he used his wisecracking humor to distance himself from his feelings.

Even though she understood this, something still bothered her.

What?

The little voice inside her, the voice she had come to
love and trust over the past few weeks, whispered to search
inside for the answer.

"Inside?" she asked the voice.

"*Yes.*"

"Inside me?"

"*Yes.*"

"But it's *Glenn* who has the problem. I don't see…"

The voice was gently insistent. "*Inside.*"

Susan considered this advice for a few seconds, then
received the understanding she was seeking. "Oh I see, you
mean *I* do the same thing *Glenn* does. I often distance
myself from my feelings. Only I use different methods. Is
that what you mean?"

"Yes, that's a part of the answer. What else?"

"I don't like myself when I do it. I feel like I'm hiding.
I call myself an emotional coward."

"Yes. Hard on yourself, aren't you."

"I suppose…but are you saying I'm *exactly* like Glenn?
He uses sarcasm. Sometimes he hurts people's feelings. I
don't do that. Sure, I hide sometimes, but I'm nicer—I just
withdraw. It doesn't feel the same."

*"Your intent is the same as Glenn's. Your intent is to
hide, and you don't like it. You don't like it when Glenn
hides, and you don't like it when you hide."*

"That's true."

With this help from her inner guidance, she admitted to
herself that she was judging something in her friend Glenn
that she judged in *herself.* Moreover, it was her self judgment that came first. In fact, the *only* reason she judged
Glenn's "hiding" was *because* she judged it in herself first.
So if she could accept her own behavior, she could accept
the same behavior in Glenn.

She sighed as she realized how hard she was on herself,

and in that moment she promised to be kinder. The key was in understanding her own behavior, for she always felt more loving towards herself when she understood—*deeply* understood—the reasons for what she did.

Susan felt better about herself...and about Glenn. They were much alike in some ways. She suddenly understood that *he* must *also* have a reason why *he* hid. Perhaps if she took the time to understand him better...

This inner work took but a second. She returned to the now moment to find Glenn staring at her, waiting for a reply to the question he had asked.

Susan relaxed, her heart opened to Glenn, and she reached over and gently touched his arm. She smiled. "The first level of healing has been completed," she said seriously.

Glenn was startled—thrown off balance—as if Susan had changed the script they had always followed. He chuckled. "Good, glad to hear it. Sometime you'll have to tell me how you did it."

"Whenever you want."

"Great. Take you up on it one of these days. But not now," he said, picking up his fork and banging it against his water glass. "Now I have some hot news. Came over the TV at the motel this afternoon. Ready?"

"Glenn honey, I do declare, sometimes I think you're more fun than one of those gossip magazines. I truly do," Vicki quipped in her best Southern accent.

Glenn enjoyed the game and he grinned. "Ready?" he asked again.

"Yes," Susan and Jeff answered in unison, joining in the fun.

"Well, it appears that our young and handsome President Tipton has decided to reform the Federal Reserve system. He wants to cut its power. He wants to cut its power *by a lot*. Interesting, wouldn't you say?"

With a smirk on his face, Jeff inquired, "So tell us, Mr. Wall Street Insider, why is that so interesting?"

"Because nobody's ever been able to control the Fed.

They've tried, but the Fed has enormous power. They print the money, and that's power folks."

Susan appeared puzzled. "But the government controls the Federal Reserve, don't they? That's why they call it the Federal Reserve, isn't it?"

Glenn shook his head. "No, Washington doesn't control it. It just *looks* like they do. They call it the Federal Reserve to throw people off the track so they won't get suspicious and ask questions about who *really* controls the money in this country. Nope, nobody controls the Fed. It's private and it's powerful—*very* powerful. They do what they want, and they do not like it when anyone even *suggests* that they be controlled. Personally, I wouldn't want to mess with those guys."

Jeff thought for a moment. "Didn't President Kennedy want to reform the Federal Reserve system?"

"Hey, very good, you remember your history. He sure did, and he was hot on their trail...but then he took that damn trip to Dallas...and that's all she wrote. Then Johnson took over and the whole thing was dropped."

"So, what's Tipton going to do?"

Susan interrupted them before Glenn could reply. "Sh! Listen!" she commanded, pointing to the large screen TV in the corner of the room.

"We repeat," the announcer intoned gravely, "this is a special news bulletin. We are getting reports of a major earthquake around Palmdale, in Southern California. The quake hit about five minutes ago. Preliminary reports put it at a 5.5 or a 5.6 on the Richter Scale. There are no immediate reports of injuries, although apparently there has been some property damage. We'll keep you posted as we receive further details. We now return you to your regular programming."

Almost instantly, a comedy show flickered onto the screen, its loud and tinny laughter reverberating off the walls of the little cafe.

Susan's hands were sweaty. She wiped them on her jeans.

"That's kinda freaky, seeing as how we were just

talking about an earthquake at the channeling. You suppose there's going to be another one?" Vicki asked, obviously worried.

"Oh, they'll have some aftershocks," Glenn responded with a laugh. "You know how it is in Southern California, they rock and roll a lot."

"No!" Susan declared. The tone in her voice caught everyone's attention. "No, this is different. This one's a warning."

Vicki now looked frightened. "A warning of what?"

"Another quake."

"You don't *know* that," Vicki protested.

Susan gazed into her friend's frightened eyes and saw there a mirror of her own fear. "Yes, I do. I wish I didn't, but I do."

"When?" Jeff wanted to know

Susan shrugged her shoulders. "I can't see that."

They ate the remainder of their meal in silence, one eye on the TV in case there was any more earthquake news; but there were no further updates.

Back at the motel, Susan took a long, hot shower, hoping to dissolve the tension in her shoulders and her neck. But the tension was deep inside, and no amount of hot water cased it.

She finished her shower, wrapped a towel around herself, and sat down at the vanity to dry her hair.

Jeff came up behind her, putting his hands on her shoulders. "Sweetie, do you think it's a good idea to make predictions like that?"

His question irritated her, although the truth was she'd been asking herself the same thing. "Why not?"

"Because you're scaring people."

Susan regarded him in the mirror. "Like Vicki?"

"Yes."

"And you?"

"No," he replied. "Well, maybe a little. I mean, if there's going to be some kind of monster quake, then yeah, I guess I'd feel pretty nervous. Wouldn't you?"

She ignored his question. "So, you believe me?"

"Damn it! *I* don't know. I don't *want* it to happen. I want things to stay the way they are. I sure as hell don't want everything turned upside down by an earthquake."

"Neither do I, but I don't think it matters what we want, things are going to happen anyway."

Jeff sighed. "That's probably true. Okay, what do we do about it?"

"I'm not sure. Maybe nothing. Maybe just let every-thing unfold the way it's meant to." It didn't sound like much of an answer even to Susan. But then what *was* the answer, except to trust that everything was as it needed to be. And to trust that they were all protected.

And a part of her believed this—believed that if they relaxed and "went with the flow" they were fine; and that if they *truly* needed to see something, like the need to move to another area to escape the devastation of a natural disas-ter like an earthquake, the information would come to them.

But something still felt unsettled inside her. What was she to do about this ability to "see" things? What was she to do, for instance, if she "saw" a quake coming? Maybe Jeff was right. Maybe she *shouldn't* say anything. Maybe it was her "stuff" to deal with. Maybe she didn't need to share what she knew with anyone else. Susan sighed. That might work with other people, but what about Jeff? If they were going to be together as a committed couple, then she had to be free to say what she knew. She had to feel free to tell Jeff *everything*. There was no other way.

She swung around on the stool, facing him. "I didn't say those things back at the cafe to upset you."

"Then why *did* you say them?"

"It's the truth as I see it...and I need to express it."

Jeff threw up his hands in frustration. "See, that's what bothers me! You never give me answers I can understand!"

"You don't understand what I just said?"

"Nope."

Following her intuition, Susan asked, "Is it because I'm not being logical?"

"Yeah. I think that's it. Give me something that makes sense...something I can *understand.*"

"So if I'm not being logical, then I'm not making any sense to you. Right?"

"Right. You sound like...what's her name, the one at the channeling?"

"Veda?"

"Yes, you sound like Veda. You're both predicting things...but you don't have any *evidence.*"

"Then why does it bother you? Why not say we're guessing, or something, and let it go at that?"

"You know why it bothers me? Because I *believe* you. Like I believed Veda tonight. I know you're telling the truth. I can *feel* it. But it doesn't make any sense. How can you and Veda know those things?"

"I understand exactly what you mean. It doesn't make any sense to me either... yet there it is."

Jeff laughed in disbelief. "You mean *you* don't understand this *either*?"

"No."

"Huh. Doesn't that bug you?"

"Sometimes it does, but I don't make a big deal of it. I mean, I don't *focus* on it, because if I do then the truth doesn't come through. And I want the truth. I want the truth more than *anything.*"

"But you don't understand how you know these things?"

Susan shook her head no.

"This may sound weird, but for some reason that makes me feel better." Looking suddenly embarrassed, he continued, "I know that probably sounds strange, but...the thing is...sometimes I feel like I don't know *anything*...and you know *everything*. I want to understand all this stuff, but..." he said, looking down at the floor.

Susan took his hand. She felt much love for this man who was her husband. He wanted to know who he was, and that made him a very special person. "Jeff, we're not going to figure this out tonight, so why not let it rest for awhile? Okay?"

"Sure, but we need to talk more. Not only about this, but about *us*. Agreed?"

"Agreed."

Susan prayed that they would both receive the understandings they desired.

After Jeff had gone to sleep, Susan lay in her bed, feeling restless and unable to sleep. She turned on the bedside lamp, picked up the copy of *Mylokos of Lemuria* that she had bought at Evelyn's bookstore, opened it to the first page and read:

> "Greetings to you my brothers and sisters. I am Mylokos of Lemuria, speaking to you from the time of 77,000 years ago.
>
> I will begin by relating to you what I see as I awake each morning. From the many windows in my round house, I see plants and flowers everywhere. The brightly colored flowers bloom with fragrances not known in your world now. The air is beautifully soft and moist, for it has rained recently, as it does so often here. As I leave my abode, I see the beautiful pool where so many in my village gather to bathe and relax in the warm water, or to lie on the soft, mossy banks. A dolphin greets me from the pool, beckoning me to come and play."

Susan put the book down and realized that she had been silently crying. Her heart ached with a memory. She knew this place of which Mylokos spoke—although she did not know how that was possible—and she yearned to be there once again, to swim in the cool, refreshing water, to play with the dolphins and the other sea creatures who came to visit, and then to lie in the warm sun.

With the book lying open on her stomach, and her tears drying on her face, Susan slept.

Chapter Seven
Dreaming the Same Dream

From *Endtimes:* "The catalyst for many
of the changes of the 90's was the emer-
gence of the truly bonded couple. This
was, usually, a man and a woman—twin
flames—coded to find each other and to
stay together despite the social consciousness pictures of reality that attempted to pull them apart. These committed couples were the pioneers—they
opened the space and they held it open
for many others."

The Stock Market reacted unfavorably to President Tipton's plan to regulate the Federal Reserve. Down forty
points the day of his announcement, and one hundred and
fifty points the following day, many in the business community pressured the President to rescind, or at least drastically alter, his reorganization plans.

The most strident voices came from the banking industry. They adamantly opposed *any* regulation of the Fed,
predicting a further deepening of the stubborn eight year
recession if the President carried out his plans.

The Federal Reserve itself was silent.

Back in her Mill Valley home after an eventful week in

Mount Shasta, Susan sat in front of the TV, one eye on the
Presidential news conference and the other on Jeff who was
busy cooking their dinner.

"Jeff, come here for a second and listen to this and see
what you think."

Jeff appeared in the doorway, an apron tied around his
waist. He continued stirring his biscuit dough as he
watched President Tipton answering questions.

"Mr. President! Mr. President!" a portly reporter in the
back row called. "Given the performance of the Market in
the past couple of days, aren't you worried that you are further undermining confidence in an already weak economy?"

The President paused a moment before answering.
Then he stared directly into the camera, the familiar Tipton
smile brightening his face. "No, Mr. Reynolds, I am not.
Purely and simply, I and my advisors believe that the
Federal Reserve desperately needs an overhaul. Quite honestly, we don't think the Fed's record during this recession
has been the best it could have been. Certainly it hasn't
been the best for this struggling economy."

A woman reporter in the first row stood up and asked,
"But Mr. President, aren't you concerned that almost no
one in the business community agrees with you?"

The President's smile did not waver. "No, I am not.
When I took this job, I knew there would be days when I
would stand alone. This is one of those days."

A network reporter was the next to question the Presi-
dent. "Mr. President, what exactly *are* your plans for the
Fed? One rumor has it that you plan to do away with the
Fed altogether. Any truth to this?"

"We will have a position paper on this in a few days.
But I can tell you this now: It's time the economic destiny
of this country was in the hands of the American people,
and right now it's not."

"That sounds like you actually might be thinking of
abolishing the Fed," the reporter persisted.

President Tipton raised his hands, stepped back from
the podium, and said, "Please give us a few days. I realize

there are lots of rumors floating around Washington, but please give us time to get the specifics worked out."

Susan turned down the TV. "What do you think?"

"I think he's stirred up a hornet's nest. So does Glenn. He says the Fed is part of an old boy network that's run this county for a long time and that they'll fight anyone who tries to change it."

Susan watched the President, his handsome, vital face so full of confidence, and she felt a twinge of fear for him. "I think you're right, lots of people won't like what he's doing."

Jeff tapped his foot playfully. "You suppose we can decide the fate of the country later? Can I put the biscuits in now? I mean, do you think you can drag yourself away from the boob tube long enough to eat dinner?"

Susan smiled. It was good to see him kidding again. He'd been moody since their return from Mount Shasta; but, to be honest, so had she. "And what if I say no?"

"Then Sam and I will absolutely gorge ourselves on the best home made biscuits anyone ever ate. Sam will love you for it."

"He does have a passion for your biscuits, doesn't he; but he can't afford to put on any more pounds, so I guess I'll come and join you."

They ate dinner in silence. Since Jeff had cooked, Susan cleaned up. She was wiping the stove when he suggested they take their coffee outside.

Susan stretched out on the chaise lounge. "Feels like summer, doesn't it."

"Mm. Except there aren't any crickets. Too early for them I guess."

"What are you thinking about?" she asked.

"Nothing in particular. Just…oh, I don't know…how everything seems turned upside down."

"You mean like the weather?"

Jeff hesitated before answering. "Yes, that…and other things."

They felt the tension between them.

Jeff sat up and stretched. "Look, maybe we need to talk. I can feel something going on. I can feel something going on in *you*, but I can't quite put my finger on it. Want to talk about it?"

Susan wished they could put off this discussion for awhile, but she knew they couldn't. "I guess so." She sipped her coffee, stalling for time, searching for the best way to say what she had to say. "I guess what it comes down to is that I want to move to Mount Shasta."

"Because of the earthquake you see happening?"

"That's part of it...but...it's also a place I need to be."

"You *need* to be there? I don't understand. Why do you *need* to be there?"

Susan knew he would ask her this question eventually, and she still didn't have an answer that satisfied her. "You may think this is silly, but the Mountain is calling me. It's my home and I need to be there. Maybe that sounds odd, but that's how I feel."

"No, I don't think it's odd. It's just I don't think the Mountain is calling *me*."

Susan very much wanted him to understand how it was for her. "Have you ever felt that way about some place, that your *destiny* is there?"

"Sure, I think that's how I feel about *this* place."

That wasn't what she wanted to hear. "Really?"

"Yes, really. I have *roots* here, whatever the hell that means. I even know some of the neighbors. I've never gotten to know my neighbors before. Our *business* is here. Those are more roots than I've ever had in my life, and I don't think I'm ready to give that up."

Susan understood. She recalled his stories of life as an "army brat," moving from base to base every two years. Then, after leaving home, how he had continued his nomadic ways, moving here and there, like a restless dog circling round and round trying to find a comfortable spot to settle.

Susan wanted to find a solution that would accommodate them both. "Maybe I could go live there for awhile to find out what's there for me. Or maybe I could find a room or a small apartment and live up there a couple of days a week."

"You mean commute between here and Mount Shasta?"

"Sure. I know lots of people who go back and forth all the time. I could get rides with them."

Jeff shook his head. "I suppose I'm being selfish, but I don't want you to do that. I like it that we live together full time. I like it that we're a family. So does Sam. He likes it that you're here and he'd miss you."

Susan tried to smile but couldn't. "Jeff, please don't get me wrong. I'm not saying I don't want to live with you. I love the life we have together, only..."

"I know, the Mountain calls you. Well, if it calls it calls. There's nothing I can do about that."

Susan felt trapped. If she stayed in Marin County, she would be abandoning herself—abandoning a truth that was just beginning to emerge within her. On the other hand, if she followed her impulse to go to the Mountain, she feared what it might mean for their marriage.

"Something tells me you've already made up your mind to go," Jeff said quietly.

Susan was afraid if she spoke she would begin to cry. She nodded, fighting to keep back her tears.

Jeff got up from his chair. "I guess I need some time alone. I'm not feeling very good about this. It feels like we're being pulled apart. Anyway, I'm going for a drive."

"Are you angry?"

Jeff shook his head. "I'm not angry, but...I have to sort things out. I'm feeling something. I'm not sure what it is. I guess I'm feeling abandoned. Something like that. Anyway, see you later."

After Jeff left, Susan lay on the lounge chair, staring into space. Sam padded quietly over and rested his big, shaggy head on the arm of her chair. She absentmindedly scratched him behind the ear.

Susan sighed. She gazed up at the stars. "Spirit, *you* take this. I don't understand what's happening or what to do, so I'm giving it to you to take care of," she whispered.

Having given everything to Spirit, her heart opened and deep within her arose a feeling of peace and calm and of the rightness of all things. Enfolded in the arms of her Spirit, she knew all was well. She stayed in this feeling for a few minutes, then picked up their empty cups and went back inside to wait for Jeff.

She straightened the room. She sat down. She wondered where Jeff was and how he was doing. Feeling restless, she picked up a couple of books, but couldn't concentrate. She played an Eric Satie tape which helped her to relax. But mostly, she waited for the crunch of tires on the gravel that would signal Jeff's return.

It was nearly 11 before he came back. She heard his car door close. Her heart raced. Would he be angry? Would they fight? She resolved that no matter what happened she would not fight.

He came in without his usual cheery greeting and flopped down in the overstuffed chair across from her. "Okay, I've decided something."

Susan felt a tightness in her chest. "Oh, I see," she said, holding her breath.

"It's like this. We're a team. Right?"

"Right."

"So, no use breaking up the team…right?"

"Right." She wanted to hug him.

"Okay, then let's put this place up for sale and look for a house in Mount Shasta. Don't ask me why, because I don't understand it. Everything in me says *not* to do this…but…I know it's right. Isn't that how you do things? When you know something is right you just *do* it?"

"Yup, that's what I do."

"You see, whatever it is you do, it's catching. What else am I going to catch from being around you?"

"How about all your heart's desires?"

He laughed. "Great, I could go for that." He shifted around, swinging one leg over the side of the chair, something he always did when he felt relaxed. "It's a funny coincidence, but last week a couple of people came in the store and wanted to know if it was for sale. Right out of the blue. They have the money, too. How about that?"

Susan smiled mysteriously. "Easily and effortlessly."

"What?"

"Oh, I'll tell you about it later."

"Anyway, you still want to do this move, right?"

"Very much."

"We should do pretty good on the house deal. Did you notice the price of houses in Mount Shasta? Almost nothing. We might even be able to take a year or two off on what we make by selling *this* place. That wouldn't be hard to take, would it?"

"I'd love it," Susan replied. Walking over to where Jeff sat, she bent over and embraced him. "And I love *you*."

"Mm, do you now," Jeff responded, obviously pleased.

"Yes, I do indeed." She held out her hand, and he took it. "I got some new massage oil yesterday. Smells great. Want to try it out?" she asked.

Jeff grinned. "We haven't done that in awhile, have we? How about if we light a candle and put on some music?"

Susan smiled happily. "Sounds wonderful. Meet you in the bedroom."

Chapter Eight
The King Must Die

Revelations: 6:8: And I looked, and beheld a pale horse: and his name that sat
on him was Death, and Hell followed
with him. And Power was given unto
them over the fourth part of the earth, to
kill with sword, and with hunger, and
with death, and with the beasts of the
earth.

The rain began at dawn, a warm tropical rain that traveled across the Pacific from the vicinity of the Hawaiian
Islands.

Huge drops splattered against Susan's bedroom window. It was a comforting sound, a sound she loved, and she
dragged her easy chair to the garden window to listen and
to watch. She closed her eyes, letting the rain-sound pull
her into a daydream. She dreamed Mount Shasta was
melting away to reveal a golden pyramid underneath, and
the energy that emanated from this golden pyramid was the
purest love she had ever experienced.

She felt Jeff's hand on her neck. She reached up and
put her hand on top of his. "Mm, isn't this rain beautiful,"
she murmured dreamily.

Jeff gently pulled his hand away. He sat on the edge of the bed, a worried look on his face.

Susan opened her eyes and saw the expression on his face. "What is it?" Fear gripped her heart. "Oh no, it isn't Sam is it?" Sam had had a narrow brush with a car the day before, and the frightening incident was still much in her thoughts.

"No, it's something else. It's the President. Someone shot him."

"*Shot* him?"

Jeff nodded.

"But who...?"

Jeff shrugged his shoulders. "Some lunatic apparently. He got Tipton while he was jogging. Then he killed a Secret Service man before they shot *him*. He's dead."

"Is Tipton dead?"

"No...well, maybe...I'm not sure. He's in a local hospital. It's on all the networks. Want me to bring the TV in here?"

"No, I'll come out. Just give me a minute." The rain now beat furiously against her window, but Susan didn't hear it. She sighed. If the President died, his young daughter, Andie, would be fatherless. That brought a sadness to her heart. And if the President died, Vice President Storr would be President...and that brought a *chill* to her heart.

Susan went out into the living room and sat down on the couch next to Jeff. "Anything new?" she asked.

Jeff shook his head. "They aren't saying much. Only that he's being operated on and that they're sending a team of surgeons from Bethesda, but..."

"But what?"

"It doesn't sound good. It feels *wrong*. The rumor is that he hasn't regained consciousness. Maybe it's only a rumor; but if it's true, it's not good."

Suddenly, the television scene shifted to the White House where Vice President Jack Storr, appearing wan and ill at ease, was preparing to speak. The Vice President stood stiffly behind the podium while cable-carrying technicians scurried in front of him. At the last minute, an aide handed the Vice President a piece of paper. He read it, nodded, then looked into the waiting television camera.

Feedback whine from the microphone drowned out the Vice President's first attempts to speak. He waited a few seconds, then tried again. "My fellow Americans, I know your thoughts and your prayers are with our President. I know mine are. I want to assure you that President Tipton is receiving the best medical care that it is possible to provide." The Vice President paused to clear his throat. "But, my friends, no matter what happens, this great country and this great government must not falter. Therefore, as of this moment, and as provided for by the Constitution of the United States of America, I am now assuming leadership of this country. I can only hope that this will be temporary. Believe me, my friends, when I tell you that I wish with all my heart that I did not have to take this drastic measure."

Susan shook her head in disbelief. "He's always wanted to be President. This is his chance," she said, turning her attention back to the Vice President.

"But like it or not," Vice President Storr continued, "it is my duty to continue in this capacity until the President is able to resume his duties." Hesitating briefly, he finished by saying, "That is all I can tell you at this time." He seemed ill at ease, his arms hanging stiffly by his side as if they didn't belong to the rest of his body.

"Mr. Vice President!" a reporter yelled from the back row.

Vice President Storr shook his head. "I realize you have questions, but this isn't the time to answer them."

"But Mr. Vice President, is there any further news about President Tipton?"

"The President is being operated on at this minute. That's all I can tell you."

"Mr. Vice President! There's a rumor that President Tipton is dead...killed instantly...and we aren't being told."

Anger flared in the Vice President's face. "That is ridiculous! I won't even comment on it!" he yelled over his shoulder as he strode quickly from the room.

When it was obvious that the Vice President was through answering questions, the picture switched to a television studio where a group of analysts began discussing the imminent arrival of the Bethesda team.

Susan walked over to the glass doors leading to the patio. She drew aside the curtains, pressing her nose against the glass like she used to do when she was a child. She had an impulse to open the doors and walk out into the warm rain.

The television picture switched again, this time to a woman reporter standing outside the Washington, D.C. hospital where the stricken President lay. "We have just been informed that at 6 AM Eastern time President Monroe Tipton has died, a victim of the assassin's bullet. Although the team of doctors worked frantically to save his life, their efforts were in vain. The President is dead...he's dead," she said, letting the microphone drop to her side in a gesture of helplessness.

Tears slid down Susan's face. "Damn," she said softly. "I didn't always agree with him, but he was a nice man."

They continued to watch the scenes flashing across the television screen. Then, turning to Jeff, Susan said, "Everything is going to change now."

"You mean with Storr as President?"

"Yes...but it's something else, too. I wish I had the words for what I am seeing. Oh, I get it...hard times. Yes, that's what it is, hard times are coming for this country."

"Oh, well, we've always survived."

"Sure, we'll survive. Only nothing is ever going to be the same again." Susan had a vision. With the President's death, something had ended—some period in history was over. The new was coming; but the new would create much fear in the land. She visioned many frightened people, for it was as if a giant wave was forming and was about to crash upon the country, sweeping away everything in its path. People would either have to learn to ride the wave or they would perish. No one would escape having to make this choice.

Susan got up and wandered restlessly around the room.

"Jeff, I want to go to Mount Shasta more than ever now. We have friends there. We can help each other understand what's coming and how to deal with it."

"Something *is* happening, isn't it? I can't quite put my finger on it, but Tipton's assassination is part of it. Know what I mean?"

"Sure."

"God, listen to it come down. A heat wave one minute, then this rain. And now the President is dead. Nothing feels *normal* anymore. It's kind of scary. And it's not over yet, is it?"

Susan came over and sat next to him. "Probably not. But everything is fine. It's like Saint Germain says, every-thing that happens, even if it *seems* weird or scary or un-wanted, is an opportunity for growth. I'm beginning to *be-lieve* that—I mean *deeply* believe it—and I feel lots better. I just need to know that things are happening for a *reason*."

"I wish I was as sure as you are."

Susan shook her head. "Lots of times I'm *not* sure, but I'm beginning to trust that there's some kind of plan operating. I don't always see much of it. Sometimes I don't see *any* of it, but I know it's there. Most of the time all I have is a feeling or an intuition. I'm beginning to value that part of me, though, and I'm letting it *guide* me. Sometimes it doesn't seem like much to go on, but that's just my logical mind saying I need *proof.*"

"Yeah. I'm familiar with *that* one."

Susan smiled. "You *do* wrestle with that logical part of yourself, don't you? Actually, you're more intuitive than you realize. You just have to practice. I'll help, and there are lots of people in Mount Shasta who will also help."

The television was showing highlights of President Tip-ton's years in office. Susan picked up the remote control and shut the television off, feeling momentarily guilty, as if she should be crying or mourning the President's death. These feelings were not in her, though, and if anything, she felt removed from the events of the morning...as if they had little to do with her. "Look," she said, "I think we need to take our minds off this for awhile. I know *I* do. How about if we start packing? I dropped by the market yesterday and got some good boxes. We could pack some of the smaller stuff. What do you think?"

"Great."

They got the boxes from the garage and packed for an hour.

Susan moved to the bookcase and started on the books. "Oh, I forgot to tell you, I talked to Evelyn yesterday. There's a great house for rent a mile or so out of Mount Shasta. She says she knows the place well and that it's perfect for us. Want to go up and have a look? We could take a few boxes with us. It would be a real beginning."

Jeff considered this for a minute. "Sure, how about tomorrow?"

Susan clapped her hands. "Let's do it!"

"By the way, how much is this place? I bet it's expensive, being out in the country and all."

"Evelyn says six hundred and fifty a month."

Jeff chuckled. "Six hundred and fifty? It's gotta be a dump. You can't even rent a *garage* for that price in *Marin County*."

Susan playfully tossed a book in his direction. "Will you quit being so pessimistic. This is going to be an easy move. Easy and effortless."

"You sure about that?"

"Yes."

Jeff retrieved the book she had thrown. "Hey, this is one of *my* books. The least you could have done is thrown one of yours."

"You deserved it."

"You think so, huh?" He smiled. "Six hundred and fifty? You sure it has indoor plumbing, being that cheap and being in the country?"

"We'll ask Evelyn tomorrow; but if it doesn't, I'll stop by the store and buy you a brand new shovel."

Chapter Nine
The Weather Changes

From *Endtimes:* "Beginning as early as the nineteen thirties, certain extraterrestrial beings began sharing technical information with Earth's secret scientific community. These elite Earth scientists began to experiment with the Planetary energy fields. They learned to control and to manipulate atmospheric conditions, and over a period of years, they changed the global weather patterns to such an extent that by the late 90's it was impossible to predict the weather in any section of the country for more than a day at a time."

They were up early Sunday morning. Susan made them a simple breakfast while Jeff loaded boxes into the car.

Vicki called just as they were about to leave. "Hi, Suze, Glenn and I thought we'd drop by a little later if that's convenient."

Susan put down the muffin she'd been munching on. "Jeff and I are on our way to Mount Shasta. I think we've found a house."

There was a slight hesitation on the phone. "That's

great," Vicki responded without any enthusiasm in her voice.

Susan heard Vicki's disappointment. "Maybe some other time. How about if I call you when we get back?"

"Mm. Sure. Have a good trip. Glenn and I will miss you. Be sure to call us now."

As Susan hung up the phone, she puzzled over the conversation. It was what Vicki *didn't* say that mystified her. Her friend was usually quite direct—blunt almost. Not this time, however. This time she had been hiding something. Susan replayed the conversation in her head, she read Vicki's energy, and then she understood what Vicki had *really* been saying.

Jeff poked his head into the kitchen. "You ready?"

"Almost. By the way, that was Vicki on the phone. Guess what? She'd love to move to Mount Shasta with us."

"Is that what she said?"

"No, but it was in her voice."

Jeff removed his round granny glasses and rubbed the bridge of his nose. "Glenn would never go for it. He didn't much like the place. Made a big point of letting me know that."

"Maybe she'll come and he'll stay."

"Uh...I doubt it. Knowing Vicki, she'd more likely tie him up and throw him in the car."

"You got *that* right," Susan laughed. "Hey, I'm ready to go. Are you going to stand there all day talking or what?"

They traveled across the Black Point cutoff on their way to I-5, the freeway that would take them directly to Mount Shasta. Sheets of torrential rain pounded down on the narrow two lane road, forcing Jeff to slow to a crawl. The rain was so heavy he had trouble seeing through the windshield.

Jeff shook his head. "I've never seen it rain so hard here. I've got the wipers on high, but they still can't keep up."

Susan noticed with some apprehension that parts of the rain slick road were beginning to flood. She hoped they would be off this stretch of highway soon. She'd never liked it—it was too narrow, the oncoming cars traveled too fast, and, because the bay came almost right up to the side of the road, there was no safe place to pull over if the need arose.

She turned on the radio to take her mind off the dangerous highway. Predictably, the news focused on the assassination of the President.

"The President's wife, Margaret, and their teenage daughter, Andie, remain in seclusion at an unspecified location," the newscaster reported. "Continuing with the awful story of this tragedy, we now have more information about the President's assassin. His name, as we reported to you yesterday, was Andrew Lentz, a thirty-six year old unemployed white male. The news services are now reporting that Mr. Lentz was a former mental patient from the State of Mississippi. We know little about the exact nature of his mental condition, only that for the past several months he had been an inmate in the state run institution for the criminally insane. He apparently has no family, although there is an unconfirmed rumor of a sister living somewhere in Georgia."

Susan leaned forward, resting her arms on the dashboard of the car. "A mental patient. Do you believe that?"

"Sure. Why not?"

"It's too pat."

Jeff slowed the car and negotiated around an area of flooded roadway. "There's lots of crazies out there."

Susan sighed. "I suppose; but it's still too predictable. It's what everyone would expect. Like, if you were going to write a movie script, you'd have this guy be a mental patient."

"So, what are you saying?" Jeff asked, picking up speed again.

Susan pushed back what she knew, afraid, at that moment, to admit it into her consciousness. "Oh, nothing I guess."

Jeff turned onto I-5 and increased speed. Susan breathed easier now that they were on the long, wide, straight Interstate. She turned her attention back to the radio.

"The motive is, of course, the missing element in this horrible tragedy. We can but guess at this now, for the only person who knows for sure was cut down in a hail of Secret Service bullets, so the truth may never be known. Meanwhile, back in Washington, President Storr has assured the nation and the world that he intends to carry on with the late President's policies."

Jeff glanced at Susan. "What do you think Storr is going to do?"

Susan shook her head. "I'm not sure. But whatever he does, Washington won't be as much fun." Although not a political person, she had liked Tipton's down-home, folksy style; and she had enjoyed it when, in the middle of his second term, he'd embarked on another one of his famous bus trips, this one a coast-to-coast trek lasting three weeks. Tipton obviously loved these trips, and they had added some lightheartedness to an otherwise dreary Washington scene. She doubted that the dour Storr would carry on with the bus trips—or anything else that was fun. He just didn't seem to understand how to enjoy himself.

"Now for some California news," the broadcaster continued. "The big story is, of course, the weather. First a heat wave in the middle of winter, now this rain. Unlike most storms this time of year, *this* one is coming straight across the Pacific and is dropping huge amounts of warm tropical moisture everywhere in the state. And the long range forecast is for more rain throughout this week and into next.

"In the Southern part of the state, officials have posted new flash flood warnings. Thus far, there are eleven reported deaths in and around the Los Angeles area. Five people died last night when a creek suddenly overflowed, sending a raging torrent of water sweeping through a low-lying trailer park. Officials say it may be days before searchers can recover the bodies. One rescue worker on the scene offered the opinion that the bodies may have washed out to sea, making recovery unlikely.

"Meanwhile, north state rivers are rising at an alarming rate. The Russian and Eel rivers are already at flood stage, and disaster officials are preparing for the worst. The amount of rain that has fallen in these two days is truly astounding: Over on the coast, Fort Bragg received 18 inches; Ukiah and Santa Rosa report in with 12 inches; and parts of Marin County have been deluged with an unbelievable 25 inches in a little over forty-eight hours. If you're thinking that these represent record amounts of rainfall, you're right."

"It's freaky," Jeff remarked. "It's like Mother Nature has gone crazy."

Susan wondered about the meaning of the unusual weather. Did it signal the beginning of the long predicted earth changes? Or was it something else?

The newscaster continued, "California does not have the only odd weather. The heat wave that blistered the Golden State two short days ago has mysteriously moved on to the Midwest. The high in Kansas City today was an unbelievable 110 degrees, while Decatur, Illinois, checked in with an even 100. And this morning the city of Atlanta was rocked by an earthquake measuring 5.9 on the Richter Scale. A spokesman for the National Weather Service has assured us that stranger periods of weather have occurred, although he didn't offer any specific details."

They passed the Apple Orchard, looking soggy and forlorn, its colorful array of flags hanging limply in the drenching rain. After a brief stop for lunch at a restaurant a few miles north of Williams, they continued on I-5 to the upper valley town of Red Bluff where they crossed the raging Sacramento River. Although not yet in danger of flooding, the river looked angry and brown and swollen and carried in its swiftly moving current bushes and tree limbs and even whole trees ripped from its banks somewhere upstream.

They picked up Evelyn, then drove out to see the house. On the way, she told them about a channeling Veda had done after the President's assassination.

"People had lots of questions. They wanted to know what it meant—the President's death and the odd weather," Evelyn said. "Saint Germain wouldn't say anything specific. He almost never does, the rat; but I got the strongest feeling he was telling us to be ready for some major shifts—some big changes."

Susan nodded. "I get that, too."

"He also discussed some astrological conjunctions that are happening now. He says these conjunctions make it an even more powerful time."

"I wish I'd been there," Susan said wistfully.

"Oh, and everyone says hello…and wants you to know they're happy as clams the two of you are moving up here. So am I of course."

"Evelyn, are you *sure* they said happy as clams?" Jeff teased.

"Their exact words, my dear."

Susan and Jeff loved the house—a modified A frame set on almost two acres of fruit trees. Although a thick blanket of gray clouds covered the Mountain, Evelyn assured them that when the clouds lifted the view from the deck would "knock their socks off."

"You say it's for sale?" Susan asked. She didn't like the idea of having to show the house to a never-ending parade of prospective buyers.

Evelyn chuckled. "Just about every place that's for rent is also for sale. It's a little game we play. As I recall, this one's been on the market a long time—three or four years. I know the agent who has the listing. She doesn't show the house much anymore, so don't worry, you're not likely to be bothered," she added, as if reading Susan's thoughts.

They explored the house and the grounds for the next hour, then returned to Mount Shasta to sign the lease. Susan wanted to stay in their new home that night, but there was no power and only bare floors to sleep on; so, reluctantly, she agreed to spend the night in a motel. They dropped Evelyn at her store, promising to say good-bye before they left for Marin County.

The next two weeks were busy ones. After putting their house up for sale, they made three more trips to Mount Shasta, the third one with a huge truck stuffed with most of their belongings. Vicki went with them on this last trip — "to take a look around," as she put it.

Meanwhile, the torrential rain persisted. The Weather Service was calling it the worst storm in a hundred years, perhaps the worst storm in the nation's history, worse than the hurricanes of 1992 or the tremendous Southwest floods of 1996. Parts of California would never be the same. The Earth had absorbed all the water She could, and the results were devastating. Much of the beautiful and scenic Highway 1, which snaked along the rugged California coastline, gave up and slipped into the ocean, a victim of the saturated earth. The California Department of Transportation had no plans to rebuild it. Rivers were changing course, and the raging water washed away thousands of homes in its path. A hundred thousand flood victims found shelter in schools and armories. Many would stay for months. Estimates for the cost of the storm and the flood damage ranged from 2 to 4 billion dollars. Two thousand people had lost their lives in storm related incidents.

To make matters worse, hordes of ants and other insects, driven to find shelter from the rising water, swarmed into homes and businesses, defying any effort to drive them out.

In Washington, President Storr continued to insist that there would be no major changes in presidential policy, although few believed him. A week after President Tipton's death, the Commerce Secretary resigned. A week later, the Secretary of Defense also left office. Neither man gave any reasons. Political insiders predicted more changes to come.

Of the late President's much publicized plan to reform the Federal Reserve, nothing more was heard.

Their move complete, Susan and Jeff settled into life in Mount Shasta. Jeff made two more trips to Marin County to arrange for the sale of their hardware store. Susan notified her book publisher of her move, and they were now sending her work to Mount Shasta. They even had a fairly solid offer on their Marin County home.

All seemed well.

While browsing in the *San Francisco Ledger*, Susan spied the following story: A retired Geophysicist living in Los Angeles speculated that the huge amount of water soaked up by the Earth could produce some serious problems. "Water is extremely heavy," he was quoted as saying. "The rain has come quickly, and there is now a tremendous weight suddenly pushing down on the California land mass. Frankly, we've never had a situation like this before," he had added.

The newspaper dismissed him as a kindly, well intentioned quack and relegated him to the back page of the paper.

Chapter Ten
Quake!

Revelations: 6:12: And I beheld when he
had opened the sixth seal, and, lo, there
was a great earthquake; and the sun became black as sackcloth of hair, and the
moon became as blood.

The California earthquake, predicted by so many for so
long, struck Southern California at 9 AM Monday morning—the worst possible time, with millions of people just
settling into work and millions of children in school.

So great was the magnitude of the quake that when the
reporting stations in Berkeley, California, and in Golden,
Colorado, received the initial reports, those monitoring the
equipment at first suspected some malfunction in the sensing devices.

Peter Gould, in charge of the Berkeley station that
morning, felt the sharp jolt of a quake a few seconds after 9
AM. Before he checked his instruments, he played a familiar game with himself, guessing the strength and the location of the tremor to see how close he could come. Most of
the time his guesses were amazingly accurate. No doubt
about it, he had a "feel" for earthquakes. Estimating this
one to be a magnitude 5 or 6, he placed it around Hollister,
an active seismic area eighty or so miles to the South.

Nothing unusual about that, even a 5 or 6 was common
around Hollister.

But Peter was not even close. This wasn't a Hollister quake. It wasn't even a Northern California quake. This quake had struck more than two hundred miles farther south, in Los Angeles.

After steadying himself, Peter looked at his machine to check his prediction. The seismograph registered a quake of magnitude 11.4.

"That's impossible," he muttered to himself. "Damn machine is on the blink." Frustrated at the apparent malfunction of the seismograph, and eager for an accurate reading, he called another, smaller seismic station on a different part of the Berkeley campus. "Hey, Jed, on that quake that just hit, something's screwed up over here. I'm getting a weird reading. What'd *you* get?"

Silence, and then, "11.4," the shaky voice on the other end of the phone answered.

Peter slammed down the phone. "Unh-unh...no way," he growled. His brain would not believe that an earthquake of magnitude 11.4 had actually occurred. He shook his head as if to clear away the imaginary cobwebs. An 11.4 quake simply wasn't possible. Peter had learned a lot about earthquakes, and he knew that there had never been such a quake in recorded history. The most violent earthquakes ever recorded — two of them — had both occurred offshore, one on January 31, 1906, off the coastline of Columbia, and the other on March 2, 1933, off the east coast of Honshu, Japan. Both measured 8.9.

An 11.4 quake wasn't possible. So, *both* machines must be on the blink. His logical mind wouldn't admit to any other possibility.

Out of habit more than anything else, he flipped on the radio. "We are getting scattered reports of a moderate earthquake located somewhere in the Bay Area. We are checking with Berkeley now to find out the magnitude and the exact location," the worried sounding newscaster said.

"You'll have to wait guys — we're busy here," Peter mumbled, picking up the special phone that connected the Berkeley lab with the USGS Station in Golden, Colorado.

"Golden!" a woman yelled into the phone.

"This is Berkeley. Say, on that quake that hit, did you folks get a reading? 5 or 6 maybe?" he asked hopefully.

"5 or 6? You must be kidding!"

"No, I'm *not* kidding. The 9 AM quake, damn it! What's your reading?" Peter barked.

"Right! 9 AM.! Looks like it might be around Palm Springs!"

"Yeah. Okay. *That* one! What's your reading?"

"A preliminary reading of 11.4! Sounds impossible, but that's what we got!" she yelled.

"Oh my God," Peter whispered as he hung up the phone.

There had never been a quake like it in human reckoning. The worst quake, for people killed, took place on January 23, 1556, in the northern province of Shensi, China. Over 800,000 people died in that tremor. The next most devastating earthquake occurred in Calcutta, India, on October 11, 1737. Although estimates vary, it appears that more than 300,000 human beings perished in that disaster.

The initial jolt from *this* quake killed 2 million people instantly. There was no warning and no chance to escape — they died where they were, crushed by roofs and walls from thousands of falling buildings, or trapped and smothered under collapsing freeways.

Added to the 2 million who died instantly, another million perished in the next few hours, doomed, in many cases, because rescue crews could not get to them in time.

Most of the city's natural gas lines ruptured. Also, most of the pipelines carrying gasoline, jet fuel, and other flammable substances. These materials quickly ignited, the fires spread rapidly, and with mountains of rubble clogging the streets, preventing fire crews from moving in their equipment, these fires raged unchecked for many hours...or, in some cases, many days.

Although by evening a few emergency crews were pushing into the inner city, most, on seeing the enormity of the devastation, and knowing they could do little by themselves, turned around and went back for more help.

An incoming jetliner about to land at LAX touched down on a runway that heaved and buckled so violently the jet flipped over like a toy, exploding in a ball of flame, instantly killing everyone on board. Seconds later, the remainder of the airport was but a pile of rubble, a victim of the violently heaving earth.

As the quake hit, three traffic copters were in the air reporting on the Monday morning commute. The reporters in these copters witnessed the destruction of their city: buildings, including the new "quake proof" high-rises, swaying and then collapsing, sending up huge plumes of dust; freeways twisting and writhing and groaning, then crashing to earth, bringing with them thousands of cars and trucks; landfill areas liquefying, sucking buildings under so quickly they might as well have been built on water. After recovering from their initial shock, the traffic spotters frantically relayed these scenes of destruction to their home stations—only no one was alive to receive their reports.

The earthquake shook the ground and rattled windows as far east as Georgia, as far South as Mexico City, and as far North as Edmonton, Canada.

Within seconds, the business district of Los Angeles ceased to exist. Not one building remained upright. Not one human being remained alive.

Ordinarily, in an earthquake or other natural disaster of similar proportions, officials issued a state of emergency. This time there was only silence. The reason why officials of the City and County of Los Angeles did not declare a state of emergency was because no officials were alive to declare it.

Hospitals and other emergency care facilities suffered severe damage. The quakes of previous years had alerted officials to the possible danger of losing these structures, and they had seismically upgraded many of the buildings. But no one had foreseen a quake of this strength. Most of the area's hospitals, including all the older ones, collapsed in the first few seconds. The few that remained could not cope with the crush of victims needing emergency medical care. The scene in the next few hours resembled a war zone, with the injured and the dying spilling out of the hospitals, onto parking lots and lawns and even sidewalks, as doctors and nurses worked feverishly to save as many lives as possible.

If the scene at the hospitals was reminiscent of a war zone, the pictures being relayed by the orbiting satellites might have come straight from a science fiction movie. These satellite photos showed huge fissures splitting open along the fault line, swallowing entire buildings and even parts of cities. They showed thousands of buildings and hundreds of miles of freeways collapsing almost simultaneously, sending a giant plume of debris shooting into the air, reminding some of the mushroom cloud produced by a nuclear explosion. And perhaps strangest of all, they showed the surface of the Earth for miles in every direction heaving and buckling and rippling, as if a race of giant burrowing animals was making its way just under the skin of the Planet.

The entire earthquake was over in less than two minutes.

Reaction from Washington was quick in coming. Moments after the quake, an anxious Press Secretary summoned President Storr from a cabinet meeting and apprised him of the disaster. He immediately declared a state of emergency, thus mobilizing the National Guard and federal troops. But it would be two full working days before any of these troops arrived at the disaster area.

A newly reorganized FEMA, now under the control of the military since the terrible Southwest flooding of 1996, was also called into action; but it, too, was slow to respond.

The wire services and the television networks picked up the story almost instantly, and by 9:30 AM most people in the United States knew that a monstrous earthquake had struck Southern California. Although details were sketchy, it was obvious that a natural catastrophe of almost unimaginable proportions had just occurred.

Some Americans, believing that Californians had too long lived in sin, secretly rejoiced at this news. In their opinion, God had punished the sinners, and they had gotten what they deserved.

Most Americans, however, did not share this view. The news of the quake shocked them—they dropped what they were doing, gluing themselves to the radio or the television, desperate for more news.

Few Americans had experienced the terror or the devastation of a major earthquake, so they had difficulty fully comprehending what had happened. Of those who *had* experienced a major quake, most simply prayed for their brothers and sisters in California.

Later that Monday, a little after 11 AM Eastern time, President Storr suspended trading on the New York Stock Exchange. He did this, in his words, "For the good of the country and to avoid further panic." The panic he referred to had occurred earlier in the day. As news of the California disaster swept through the board rooms of the country's major corporations, and through Wall Street itself, the Market reacted with blind panic, losing 500 points—nearly one sixth of its entire worth—in less than twenty minutes. It was to avoid a total collapse of the Market that prompted the President to suspend trading for the day.

Wall Street was not the only place to feel the cold grip of fear. The nation's insurance companies were quick to grasp the implications of the California quake, and they did not like what they saw. The nineties had not been kind to the insurance companies. The inordinate number of natural disasters had forced them to dig deep into reserve funds, and many were now teetering on the edge of ruin. Faced with the prospect of billions of dollars in claims sure to come from the California quake, claims they knew they could not pay, they decided to throw themselves on the mercy of the United States Government—they would ask Washington to absolve them from having to pay for the quake damage. Failing that, most were seriously considering bankruptcy.

As this frantic activity was taking place in New York

and elsewhere, a curious calm spread over the southern half of California.

But then, for all practical purposes, Southern California had ceased to exist.

Chapter Eleven
The Quake is Felt in Mount Shasta

Revelations: 8:12: And the fourth angel
sounded, and the third part of the sun
was smitten, and the third part of the
moon, and the third part of the stars; so
as the third part of them was darkened,
and the day shone not for a third part of
it, and the night likewise.

Although the earthquake was felt in Mount Shasta, it
was experienced as a moderate jolt. Most Mount Shastans
estimated it to be a quake of magnitude 5 or so and nothing
to be overly concerned about. However, as people learned
the *real* magnitude of the Los Angeles tremor, a quiet panic
gripped the community.

News of a major disaster travels fast in a small town. In
Mount Shasta, as in many towns and villages across California and across the nation, people gathered in little knots
on street corners, in shops, and in cafes, sharing what news
they had and hungry for more. Almost everyone in Mount
Shasta had friends or relatives in Southern California...adding to their frantic need for more information.

Soon after the quake hit, the rumors began to spread:
Huge chunks of Southern California had broken off and
had fallen into the Pacific Ocean; the Diablo Canyon

Nuclear Power Plant, located near San Luis Obispo, about a hundred miles from the epicenter of the quake, had ruptured and was in meltdown; another more powerful quake was about to hit—the scientists knew about it and they were withholding the information.

Was there truth to any of these rumors? California was still in one piece—for now—although a huge portion of the landmass in Southern California had sunk more than 6 inches. Safety inspectors at the Diablo Canyon plant *did* detect cracks at several key places, but for some unexplained reason did not report this to the proper authorities for several days. And some scientists, privy to information most Americans did not have access to, did indeed know more than they were publicly admitting—concerning earthquakes...and many other aspects of American life.

Susan and Jeff were enjoying breakfast at the Sunshine Cafe when the earthquake hit. For fifteen seconds, the hanging lamps swayed and the tables shook; then everything was eerily still.

Susan wiped up her spilled coffee. Her stomach churned and her heart raced as she understood, intuitively, what had just happened.

"Wow!" someone yelled. "Was that an explosion? Are they blasting around here? What the hell *was* it?"

"It was an earthquake," Susan replied, with more calmness than she truly felt.

"You sure?"

"Yes."

"Around here? From inside the Mountain? Is the Mountain going to erupt?"

"It was farther away," Susan answered.

Someone turned on the small portable television, but the cable was out. They waited. The usually noisy and bustling cafe was strangely quiet.

Cable service resumed three minutes—three very *long* minutes—later. The television screen flickered to life, catching an obviously shaken newscaster in mid sentence, "...on the twentieth floor here in San Francisco and I can tell you the building swayed pretty good. In fact, it's still moving around. It's not an experience I want to go through again." He swallowed hard. "I sure hope that's the only one we're going to get." He paused, glancing nervously around. Then, appearing to regain his composure, he continued, "Okay now, we don't have any information yet about possible damage or loss of life, but we'll pass it along to you as soon as it comes in. We're staying on the air round the clock if we need to, folks. To repeat, for those of you who might have missed it, at 9 AM this morning an earthquake of magnitude 11.4 struck the area around the City of Los Angeles. And we *do* have confirmation on that magnitude. Apparently that's correct. It...it doesn't sound possible, though, so we're going to check that figure again. It doesn't seem like that could be possible," he repeated in a stunned voice. He stopped again, wiping the perspiration from his forehead, making no attempt to hide this from the all-seeing eye of the television camera. "The news is likely to be bad, folks. We're trying to get a feed from Los Angeles, but no luck yet. Stay tuned."

Susan got up and hurried to the pay phone in the back of the cafe. A bearded, middle aged man, one of the cafe regulars, was just hanging up. He shook his head. "No phone. Nothing. All outside lines are down."

Susan nodded and returned to join Jeff.

A worried man at the next table asked, "11.4? How could that be? It doesn't sound right." He glanced around to see if anyone could help him. "How big was the Alaska quake? You know, the *big* one?"

No one was quite sure. A woman guessed, "8.1 or 8.2 or something like that?"

"So an 11.4, how much stronger would that be? Wouldn't it be thirty times as strong? Or is it 300? It *couldn't* be 300...it *couldn't* be," the man said softly, his eyes suddenly filling with tears.

Another man added this, "Hell, even if it was only thirty times, I mean, my God, you know what that would be like? Ever see pictures of that Alaska quake? And thirty times that? Holy shit."

Yet another woman said, "My cousin was in that quake. Got tossed around pretty good. Broke his leg. Lost his sense of balance for six months after that."

"Stop it! Please stop it!" the young woman on Susan's left demanded tearfully. Reaching over and putting her arm around her, Susan asked, "What's the matter?"

It took the woman a moment before she could speak. "I have a brother in Los Angeles," she sobbed. "I just talked to him the other night. He's going to get another job...a really good one. He lives right in Los Angeles. He isn't dead is he?"

Susan looked into the woman's frightened eyes and patted her on the shoulder. It was all she could think of to do. "We don't know anything yet. We have to wait. We just have to wait."

"He *couldn't* be dead. Maybe they're wrong. Maybe it wasn't that strong. Maybe they're wrong," the woman said hopefully.

Forcing a smile, Susan said, "It's best to wait. Can I get you some tea? Would you like some tea?"

The young woman didn't hear her. In a dazed voice, she continued, "But he couldn't be dead. His birthday is next week. I just bought him a present. It's a wall clock for his study. He couldn't be dead."

Evelyn and Anna, who had been watching this scene, walked over to Susan's table.

Anna gently put her hand on the sobbing woman's shoulder. "Karen, what's the matter? Can you tell us?"

"It's my brother. He...he lives in Los Angeles."

Evelyn and Anna and Susan exchanged glances. An understanding on a very deep level passed between them, an understanding that they probably could not have consciously voiced in that moment.

The newcomers pulled their chairs up to the table, one on either side of Karen. They put their arms around her, and, with the loving energy of the three women pouring into her, Karen relaxed.

They sat quietly, staring vacantly at the television.

Cable service was disrupted three more times in the next fifteen minutes.

Jeff was the first to speak. "Look, hon," he said to Susan, "what if I take the car and go home and call Vicki and Glenn? Maybe if I keep trying I'll get through. I'd like to find out if they're okay. And I'd kind of like to see if our old house is still in one piece," he added with a nervous laugh.

"Sure."

"Great. Be back as soon as I can."

The group sharing Susan's table watched the television—when it was working. They talked softly among themselves, voicing their fears and reassuring each other as best they could. When a newcomer entered the tiny cafe, they looked up expectantly, hoping for more news, but there was none.

Jeff returned two hours later, shaking his head. "Phones are still out," he said, joining Susan and the others at the table.

They lingered at the cafe for awhile, making small talk and keeping each other company. Then Susan invited the group back to their home. After a simple dinner, they returned to their television vigil. The networks were now broadcasting a few pictures of the quake damage. No one talked as these images of devastation flashed across the screen.

The scene shifted to the Governor's news conference in Sacramento. Susan had never liked this man. No one appeared to notice when she turned off the sound.

"It's the beginning of the Earth changes," Anna stated.

"Why do so many have to die?" Karen asked. Although she had calmed down considerably from the morning, the worry and the pain were evident in her voice.

Evelyn smoothed Karen's hair. "They chose to be there for reasons we may never understand," she said gently, obviously selecting her words carefully.

Much to everybody's surprise, Karen nodded, as if agreeing with Evelyn. "But why so many?" Karen asked, for it was now clear to everyone that millions had perished in the quake.

"Maybe it's the only way the rest of us will wake up," Evelyn replied. "We *must* wake up you know, because our Mother Earth is saying she can't take any more abuse. She must heal. Sometimes the healing looks violent...and I guess it is, but...sometimes it's the only way."

Anna took Karen's hand. "What's your brother's name?"

Karen's eyes instantly filled with tears. "Tom. His name is Tom. He's my kid brother. I used to call him Tommy, but he hated it, so I quit calling him that. I guess he got all grown up."

"Sure. Well, whatever's happened, it's Tom's healing, too. I guess that sounds strange, but it's the truth."

"No, it doesn't sound strange. I guess I know that, but it's still hard to take."

As Susan watched Anna console Karen, she remembered someone telling her that Anna also had family in Los Angeles—a sister she thought. How was Anna dealing with her own pain? Then Susan understood that what Anna was saying to Karen she was also saying to herself.

The little group spent the rest of the evening huddled around the television. Jeff made two trips to the wood pile for more wood. Around midnight, Susan heated up the soup she and Jeff had made the day before. It was after 2 AM when the last person left for home.

Chapter Twelve
The Aftermath

From *Endtimes*: "Those whose dream it
was to control Earth saw in the
California earthquake of 1997 many
opportunities to bring their plans to
fruition."

For twenty-two days the warm tropical rain had contin
ued its relentless drenching of California. The rain had
poured down for so long and had caused so much damage,
that now, when whole blocks of houses slid down rain-slick
hills, or when those living in low-lying areas fled for their
lives from flash floods, no one noticed—it simply wasn't
considered news anymore.

The rain also severely hampered relief efforts in Los
Angeles. With almost no freeways left standing, the relief
and rescue vehicles had to negotiate flooded streets, or
streets horribly twisted and buckled by the quake. Often,
the rescue teams made their own way, striking out cross-
country, ignoring the streets altogether.

On Wednesday afternoon, two days after the quake,
disaster officials declared martial law from Bakersfield to
the Mexican border. The official blockade began at the tiny
valley town of Wheeler Ridge, situated on I-5, 30 miles
South of Bakersfield. Only National Guard and federal

troops had the right to move past this point and into the re-stricted zone. No one else was allowed in or *out* of this area.

Anyone traveling South along one of the major Cali-fornia freeways, or on one of the many secondary roads, met a cordon of troops and tanks guarding this imaginary North-South border. At several checkpoints along this line, the border patrol halted travelers, politely but firmly in-formed them that the stricken area was off limits, then turned the motorists around and headed them back towards Northern California.

Of course, many more people wanted to leave the earthquake zone than to enter it. Military Intelligence esti-mated that on the Wednesday after the quake more than 500,000 people attempted to flee into Northern California; but the border troops also halted these quake "refugees."

The troops guarding these checkpoints gave no reasons for their actions.

Many earthquake victims did not take this blockade se-riously. Dazed and in shock and often in need of medical attention, they argued and pleaded with the soldiers to let them through. When it was clear that the border patrol would not allow them into Northern California, many vic-tims attempted to run the blockade. The troops had their orders, however, and their orders were to seal off the area tightly. They warned the would-be blockade runners...but only once. If the refugees persisted in their attempts to cross, the soldiers shot them or they blew up their cars. The twisted, smoking wreckage of these vehicles soon littered the freeways. These sobering scenes convinced many that the military meant business, and the number of attempted crossings diminished greatly over the next few days.

Some people, of course, successfully crossed the bor-der; but these were hardy souls who avoided the freeways and the secondary roads, crossing over in open country instead, taking advantage of the more than 200 miles of sparsely populated territory, much of it mountainous, stretching from the Pacific Ocean to the Nevada border.

In the first few days after the quake, the border troops

could not effectively patrol this huge area; but, by the following Monday, using helicopters and a fresh infusion of personnel, they sealed the border tight, slicing the State of California in half.

Farther south, units of the Mexican Federal Army guarded their own border. They, too, had orders to use whatever force was necessary to ensure that no one crossed into their territory.

Very few citizens protested this action by the United States Military. Perhaps, to most Americans, a military blockade, even one that resulted in hundreds of civilian deaths, did not seem very important compared to the tremendous loss of life and the almost unbelievable destruction of the California quake. Or, perhaps it was that most Americans had for so long given their power away to the government that they simply did not question the military's harsh tactics.

A few congress people—six congressmen and two congresswomen—*did* question this killing of unarmed civilians; but after a White House meeting with President Storr, the Joint Chiefs of Staff, the Cabinet, and the CIA, the eight members of Congress officially withdrew their protests. They gave no reasons for their decision.

The other group to protest was Amnesty International. They denounced the civilian casualties and threatened lawsuits. The major newspapers carried reports of this protest for a couple of days. Then they dropped the story.

Embarrassed perhaps by the negative attention, the military acted swiftly to quell any further protest. On Friday, four days after the earthquake, citing unspecified reasons of national security, they imposed a complete news blackout. The new regulations forbid reporters to be inside the quake area or within 10 miles of the blockade zone itself. The regulations also prohibited the soldiers from talking to these reporters. Transgressors were summarily court-martialed.

However, the American public's need for news of the quake proved stronger than the military's need to protect its reputation. The military command succumbed to public

pressure, amending the news blackout to allow a carefully
selected corps of reporters and other media people limited
access to the quake area. However, all news coming from
the area was subject to military censorship.

   To millions of American citizens watching the 10 o'-
clock news or reading the daily paper, something about the
California earthquake didn't add up.
   On the one hand, the numbers being reported by disaster agencies painted an almost unbelievably grim picture.
Estimates of casualties mounted daily. By Saturday, the official count was 4.5 million killed and another 2 million
missing or otherwise unaccounted for. These were stagger-
ing numbers, and they did not include the millions left
homeless and in need of food and water.
   On the other hand, the *news* stories emanating from the
quake area and the interviews of quake survivors shown on
television tended to be upbeat. Too upbeat for some. They
portrayed a people who, although hard hit by adversity,
were nevertheless confident of the future; they pictured
people eager to rebuild their shattered communities; and
they portrayed people who were sure their fellow Americans would help, as they had so generously helped many
disaster victims in the past.
   Could people who had just experienced the worst
earthquake in recorded history be that optimistic?
   True, Americans are a hardy lot and tend to view the
future in positive terms. But still, the tone of these post
quake interviews did not match the terrible destruction that
had taken place.
   Reconciling these very different pictures of reality
proved troublesome for many.

   Americans all across the country avidly watched these
quake related news programs. Not everyone believed them,
however.
   For the past several weeks, Susan had grown increas-
ingly cynical about the media. She now assumed that they
were attempting to manipulate her; and based on what she

was later able to discover, she was right. It became something of a game with her to spot the manipulation—the "big lie" and the "big sell job"—as she called it.

It was with this attitude that she watched a news update on the earthquake. Federal troops, many wearing the distinctive red and blue FEMA armbands, were setting up an emergency shelter for victims who had reportedly been near the quake's epicenter. The troops, clean cut and well groomed, had just finished erecting a field kitchen. Outside, a line of families waited patiently for food. Images of quiet, somber children filled the screen.

On an impulse, Susan looked closely—*very* closely—at the children. They appeared nervous and ill at ease. Two of them, their eyes downcast, appeared to be listening to someone off camera. Was somebody giving them directions on how to look and how to behave?

Susan felt a familiar feeling in her solar plexus—*someone was lying to her.*

"Does this seem right to you?" she asked Jeff. "If you step back and take a look at the whole scene, isn't there something odd about it?"

"Yeah, but I can't quite put my finger on it."

Susan took a deep breath and asked for the truth of what she was seeing. "They don't seem normal."

"Not normal?"

"I mean they look kind of unhappy... and I guess *that's* normal... but they don't look very stressed."

"Okay, but..."

"No, think about it," Susan insisted. "Watch the kids. These are kids who have just been through the worst quake in history. They've probably seen people killed. Maybe even their parents or their brothers or sisters. They're stressed, right? Except they don't seem very upset. See any kids crying?"

"Huh. Now that you mention it, that is kind of odd."

"Or anyone throwing a temper tantrum?"

"Nope."

"What's going on here?"

"Maybe kids recover quickly from stress."

"Maybe...maybe, but that doesn't explain it."

"Shock?"

"I don't think so," she said, drawing on her own experience as a counselor for a battered women's shelter. "Shock looks different."

"Then what?"

She ignored his question. "And doesn't it look like someone is talking to the children off camera?"

Jeff peered hard at the television. "Could be. But I'm not sure."

Susan was quiet. She sent her consciousness back down to her solar plexus, and she got the same message back: *someone was lying to her.*

Susan cupped her chin in her hands. "It reminds me of an advertisement—a poorly done advertisement."

More pictures flashed across the television screen.

The screen showed the once glum looking children, now with happy faces, digging into huge, steaming plates of food.

The screen showed relaxed and smiling FEMA workers cleaning up. Susan could almost hear them whistling as they worked.

The screen showed another group of children and adults lining up outside waiting to be fed, all with the same nervous, self-conscious look about them.

Susan still did not believe what the television images wanted her to believe.

The camera cut to a close-up of the well-known TV anchorwoman who was narrating the show. Her sincere, smiling face filled the screen. "It's obvious FEMA is much more organized since being taken over by the military," she said. "This kitchen was up and running in a matter of hours. It's also obvious that these unfortunate quake victims greatly appreciate FEMA's efforts—you have only to look at the smiling faces of these children to know that." She paused and gazed directly into the camera, brushing her windblown hair out of her face. "But there is a fear among these dedicated relief workers. They fear that the scope of this disaster will eventually overwhelm FEMA's resources. FEMA will need more money—much more money." She paused to let her words sink in. "Money to buy the emergency supplies to meet the needs of these earthquake victims. Money to begin the rebuilding of shattered communities. Money to restore broken lives. How much money?" She shrugged her shoulders. "No one knows. But as you look into the eyes of these innocent children, we are sure that you and other Americans will give generously. It is, after all, the American way." She smiled. "This is Sandy Kim, somewhere on the outskirts of what was once the city of Los Angeles, signing off for now."

Susan sat back and took a deep breath. The program she had watched had attempted to manipulate her. It had attempted to make her feel *guilty*. Why? What was the purpose in making the audience feel guilty? Of course! It was a set up. Later, someone would use the stirred up guilt, would *play* on it to get something they wanted. What did they want? She nodded as the understanding came to her. She was right. The whole thing *was* an advertisement...an advertisement for money, an enormous amount of money, more money than anyone could even imagine.

She had a vision: She saw a green river of money; and the green river of money turned into a red river of blood; and the blood was the life blood—the life force—of the country...a great river of it, seeping slowly into the dry, parched ground, until none was left.

Susan trembled. The county was in grave danger. The sharks—those human beings who hid in the shadows and who lived off the misery of others—had spotted food and were circling to feed. They would attack soon, sooner than anyone knew. The feeding frenzy would bring more sharks...and more...and more.

Could the country survive? At that moment, Susan doubted it.

Chapter Thirteen
The King Needs Gold

Revelations: 18:2: And he cried mightily with a strong voice, saying, Babylon the great is fallen, is fallen, and is become the habitation of devils, and the hold of every foul spirit, and a cage of every un-clean and hateful bird.

On Saturday, President Storr, along with Governor Walker of California and federal relief officials, flew over the stricken Los Angeles area. They allowed no cameras and no reporters.

On returning to Washington, the President again ex-pressed his sympathy for those in Southern California, promising that the country would do everything it could to help. However, his short speech gave no specifics concern-ing what a long-term relief plan might look like. To the re-porters who wanted more details, or more current news of the quake itself, the President replied curtly that they would have to be patient. "We have just assembled a Presidential Task force to study the situation and to recommend a plan of action. You must wait for their report," he had stated.

Meanwhile, the floor of the New York Stock Exchange remained dark and silent. The Chicago Board of Trade and the other exchanges across the country had also suspended trading. No one knew when they would resume business.

Other world markets had also halted trading as worried foreign investors and nervous government officials took time out to gauge the impact of the California quake on their own economies.

The dollar amount of the quake damage? No one was even guessing.

Meanwhile, the rain continued to beat down on California. The already saturated ground could hold no more water; the runoff collected in large pools, and the pools turned into ponds and then into great inland lakes. To make matters worse, the vast network of dams built to provide flood control were full and were releasing water at a furious rate, adding to the already serious flooding in the downstream areas.

Unusual phenomena continued to plague other parts of the country as well. Another earthquake, this one measuring 6.2, jolted Atlanta. Disaster officials advised residents to stockpile food and water—just in case. Less intense earth tremors rattled windows and knocked cans from grocery store shelves on the Eastern Seaboard. And the Midwest baked under searing, summer-like temperatures.

On Monday, the one week anniversary of the great quake, President Storr issued an announcement forever changing the course of United States history.

"My fellow Americans," a tired and drained President Storr began, "as you are aware, one week ago today the mightiest earthquake in recorded history struck the state of California, causing tremendous losses of property and human life. Added to this, several freak storms have inflicted catastrophic flood damage throughout the area. Of course, we want very much to help our fellow citizens, but the enormity of these two disasters has strained our ability to offer the necessary assistance.

"Now, in a normal, robust economy we would have no problem responding to these disasters. This great country has weathered many such storms before. But the fact is, the reserves we *would* have had in a healthier economic climate are, regrettably, not available."

The President paused. Many in the audience shifted nervously in their seats, as if at least some of those assembled had an intuition of the bomb the President was about to drop.

The President continued, "I have been meeting around the clock with my Cabinet, with relief officials, and with the Presidential Task Force studying this calamity. It is my unpleasant duty to inform you that, due to the enormous projected costs of the reconstruction work, *and* our own lack of economic recovery, we cannot pay for relief efforts in the State of California."

There were audible gasps and some nervous laughter from the audience. A reporter in the first row yelled out, "Mr. President, are you saying…"

The President raised his hand, signaling for quiet. "This is difficult enough. Let me finish…please." Reluctantly, the reporter sat back down, and the President resumed, "Fortunately, we have many friends. In the past few days I have heard from every major world government, and all, without exception, have offered to help. Generous as these offers are, however, they fall far, far short. The immediate relief costs, together with the estimated long-range reconstruction costs, are quite likely to be in the trillions of dollars, and…"

"Did you say trillions?" the same front row reporter asked incredulously. "Surely, Sir, you must mean billions."

Being interrupted a second time visibly upset the President. "No, it's *trillions*," he snapped back, unable to conceal his irritation. "That is our best guess at this time." He gripped the podium with both hands, the muscles in his neck taut. "You must understand, we have never had such a disaster. Half of the State of California is gone, wiped out."

"It can't be trillions. Our whole federal budget is only…Ah…"

"It's a little under 2 trillion for this year!" someone yelled out.

"Okay, so are you saying that the cleanup costs will exceed what this government spends in an entire *year*?"

"I am afraid so. Now, can you see the *gravity* of this situation?"

A woman reporter asked, "You say we don't have the funds to help them...but we can't abandon them, can we, the people in California I mean?"

The President smiled, almost as if he had been waiting for this opening. "No, of course we won't abandon them. Nor do we have to, for we have just received a generous offer of help. This morning, I met with representatives from the World Bank, the International Monetary Fund, and a consortium of world bankers. They have agreed to loan us the funds to meet this emergency. Of course, this will take congressional approval, but frankly I don't see that we have any choice, and I trust the Congress will see it the same way."

Someone in the Press Corps asked a question that brought titters from many of his peers, "Mr. President, are you saying we're *broke?*"

The President flushed. "No, of course not. Of course I'm not saying we're broke."

"Then what *are* you saying?"

"I am simply saying that, due to circumstances beyond our control, we need help."

"But, Sir, isn't this really the responsibility of the private sector? Aren't the insurance companies liable for most of the costs here?"

"Under normal circumstances, yes." The President stopped and bent over in a sudden paroxysm of coughing. He drank from the glass of water on the podium. "However, the insurance companies have informed me that they cannot meet their obligations. They have requested a special waiver in the case of the California disasters, and I have granted it. Remember, the sluggish economy has hurt them...as it has all of us. And, due to the hurricanes and the floods, they have had enormous and unusual claims made on them in the past few years. No, I am afraid they do not have the means to help with this disaster."

From the back row came a question that would trouble many in the coming days, "You say we need to borrow trillions of dollars. This is an enormous sum of money. It's so huge it's almost inconceivable. What do these agencies—the world bankers and the others—what do they want in return for this loan?"

The President shrugged his shoulders. "I don't know; we will have to wait. We hope to have an answer in a few days." Then, without another look at the audience, the President turned around and abruptly left.

Although the Presidential news conference had answered *some* of the nation's questions, a host of others remained.

Many Americans, if they thought about it at all, wondered about these international agencies. Who were they? The World Bank and the International Monetary Fund were mysterious entities to most Americans. And the international bankers the President referred to, who were *they*? Which banks did they control? What were their motives for loaning the money? Who did *they* answer to, if anyone? No one seemed to have the answers to these questions. The men controlling these international organizations remained in the shadows, refusing to reveal their true identity.

Many also questioned the advisability of such a loan, likening it to a private citizen borrowing on his credit cards to pay off his other credit cards. Dangerous and shortsighted. Was there truly no other way to raise the needed capital?

One noted liberal economist posed a very intriguing question: The United States already owed a huge national debt, most of it to these same international bankers. Now, with these new loans, the debt would be even greater. What would happen, he wondered, if these international agencies called in their loans? The United States didn't have the cash or the gold reserves to repay even one *tenth* of what she owed. So if these groups *did* call in their loans, would She declare bankruptcy, like some impoverished third world country?

Glenn was pondering the same questions as he and Vicki pulled into Susan and Jeff's driveway. Although ostensibly here "just for a visit," Vicki had made it known that she planned to move to Mount Shasta, with or without Glenn...so the "visit" was, in reality, a house-hunting expedition.

"Hey, by the way, we went by your old house, and it's still standing," Glenn joked, as they settled themselves around the wood stove. He and Vicki had not been so lucky. After the earthquake, large, ominous cracks had appeared along the entire length of the foundation of their two story, Mill Valley home. Glenn took this in stride, but for Vicki it was one more reason to move.

"Great," Jeff said, the sarcasm evident in his voice. "The house is standing, but nothing's going to sell in the Bay Area now. In fact, I hear everyone is getting out as fast as they can."

Glenn nodded. "People are afraid the "big one" is going to hit San Francisco."

"Besides, who's going to buy houses now that the government's broke?" Jeff added unhappily.

Glenn laughed. "We aren't quite broke...yet; but the way Storr is going we soon will be. It's insane what he's doing."

"He has to do *something*, doesn't he?" Vicki asked. "People in California need help. He *has* to borrow the money."

Glenn took a minute to reply. "I suppose... but I've been around money my whole life. Something about this loan doesn't *smell* right."

Susan would always remember what happened next. As the three of them discussed recent events, she removed herself from the conversation. That was nothing new—she often tuned in and out of conversations going on around her. Only *this* time she lost the sense of even being in the same *room*. She did not hear them. She did not see them. She had turned her sight inward.

When asked about it later, the best she could say was that she went through a doorway into another dimension—

a dimension within her own being—and that she showed herself the great truth called Illusion.

This inner trip, which Susan likened to a waking dream, lasted but a few seconds, but it forever transformed her life.

Chapter Fourteen
Susan's Revelation

From *Endtimes:* "Millions of Light Beings had incarnated on Mother Earth to
assist in Her transformation. They had
come to help transform Her from a place
of darkness to a place of light—to create
a "Heaven on Earth."

They had also come to allow love and
joy in their own physical lives.

The two transformations—the Planetary and the personal—were the same.

The transformations required that the
physical human beings who had incarnated onto Mother Earth awaken to Divine Truth—they needed to remember
who they were and why they had come
here. The exact time of this awakening
was, for each being, wholly in the hands
of Spirit, and Spirit was, as usual, mysterious and unpredictable."

To an outside observer, the living room scene would
have appeared quite normal—four friends gathered around
a crackling fire, while outside the rain drummed on the roof
and splattered noisily against windows. In this case,

however, appearances were deceiving, for although Susan's physical body was in the room, sitting on the couch, her consciousness had flown deep within her being.

Susan saw and heard nothing of the next few moments of the conversation.

While on her inner journey, she opened to receive many truths. It was a *remembering* of what a part of her had always known.

She realized that everything that was happening—the recent Earth changes, the assassination of President Tipton, the economic crisis—was a playing out of the drama involving the Forces of Light and the Forces of Darkness.

She also realized that she had never truly understood this drama, for the veils had obscured the clarity of her vision. Now it was time for the veils to drop...and for her to see the *truth*.

Susan didn't believe in the devil—or even in the idea of evil—but she *did* believe in the Dark Forces. She wasn't sure who they were, for they shunned the light, kept out of the public eye, and preferred to hide. She also knew that many of the Dark Forces had come to Earth, that they were often in positions of power, and that *they had a vision of complete and total world domination*.

Furthermore, she believed that she and others were battling the Dark Forces. Because these Dark Forces were powerful beings, she needed to be wary. How wary? Was her life in danger? Perhaps, although she was not entirely clear on this point.

Because these were uncomfortable feelings, she usually either ignored them... *or*, she pretended she was above the battle. Of the two strategies, she preferred the latter—she pretended that she was merely a spectator and that she didn't really care who won. Neither tactic worked, however, for her Spirit *wanted* her to understand the truth; and because Spirit wanted her to understand, it pushed her to do the work that would remove the veils.

What she understood in her few seconds of brilliant inner knowing was that the Light and the Dark were the same. The *very same*.

This changed everything.

She saw it was a game—a Divine Game. Some had chosen to play the part of the Light, and some had chosen to play the part of the Dark. In other lifetimes, the roles had been reversed.

Did the players realize it was a game? Most did not. Most had even forgotten their original agreement to play the game. Indeed, they *needed* to forget. If the players remembered their Divine Origins too soon, they might not take the game seriously. If they did not take the game seriously, they would not learn what they had come to Earth to learn. So they needed to forget...and then they needed to *remember*.

It was a game, a dance, and a Divine Drama... *and she was right in the middle of it.*

She saw many other lifetimes when she had "worked" for the Dark Forces, and she knew that she might again. Only now she was "working" for the Light. It made little difference, though, which side she was on, for the Light and the Dark were simply two sides of a Divine Whole. Because they were two sides of a Divine Whole, they *defined* each other—they *needed* each other. And because they were two sides of a Divine Whole, they were both "good." Understanding this, she also understood that *the separation into Light and Dark was but an illusion, a necessary illusion, but still an illusion.*

Did this change her attitude toward the "battle" between Light and Dark? Yes, because given that she was both the Light *and* the Dark, then, on the deepest level, she was literally *both* sides of the battle. She was playing the game with herself, was *battling* herself, and *thus had only herself to fear*. The only trick, her inner guidance gently informed her, was to understand these truths on the deepest level, to bring them into consciousness in *this* lifetime, and to *live* them. The last part was the hardest, but she was confident she could do it.

Suddenly, it was humorous to her to know there were no "good" guys and no "bad" guys, and that there never had been. She grinned.

Vicki noticed her smile and was about to ask her about it, but something Glenn said diverted her attention, and she didn't follow through on her impulse.

Before Susan returned to "join" her friends, her inner guidance gently reminded her:

> *"There are no enemies.*
> *Duality is an illusion.*
> *There is only One."*

The same voice also whispered:

> *"Be patient with those you love,*
> *for they have yet to awaken to*
> *the wondrous understandings*
> *you have given yourself."*

Susan felt a surge of energy. Her understandings—her *remembering*—had released energy into her body, into her *cells*, and the energy needed expression. It needed release. It needed to *move*.

This expression had to be physical. She could yell or shout or even cry...it didn't matter...almost *any* physical expression would move the energy.

She chose to laugh. She laughed at the illusions that were so much a part of life on Mother Earth—and at herself for taking them so seriously. She laughed at the illusion that she was on the "good" team, and that others, like President Storr, were on the "bad" team. She laughed at the very idea that she was in any danger from the Dark Forces, for the Dark Forces were *her*. She laughed until the tears rolled down her cheeks and she almost couldn't breathe.

Susan's laughter was the laughter of her Spirit—it was from her belly and it was infectious. Jeff and Glenn and Vicki also had grins on their faces, although they could not have said why. They sat there, grinning broadly and staring at her.

Glenn knitted his brow quizzically. "Did I say something funny? I didn't realize that the subject of the Federal Reserve was so amusing."

His remark sent Susan into another paroxysm of laughter.

"Hon? What is it?" Jeff asked. "Mind sharing the joke?"

Susan now had the challenging task of translating what she had learned on her deep, inner journey into her conscious mind...and *then* of finding the words that would clearly convey it to her friends. The best she could do was to say, "It's not real the way we think it is. We're taking it too seriously." She just got these words out before she burst out laughing again.

"What's not real?" Glenn asked.

She waved her arm to indicate everything in front of her. "This," she giggled.

Jeff looked mystified. "I still don't get it."

"Here we are, sitting around getting worried about Storr and his policies and the weather and the Federal Reserve. We're taking it too seriously. It's a game we've agreed to play. Only we're not having much fun playing it."

Glenn raised his eyebrows in dramatic fashion. "Did you two smoke something before we got here?"

"It's not like that," Susan protested. "No drugs. Who needs *drugs*? It's funny enough *without* drugs."

They stared at her, concerned and confused, expecting her to come up with a more reasonable explanation.

Seeing the fear in their faces, she fell from her place of laughter and joy.

A childhood memory flashed into her consciousness: When she was nine, she had climbed the apple tree in her parent's front yard, had sat on one of the branches, joyful and on top of the world, then had slipped and fallen onto the hard cement, all joy gone. It had been a painful experience to have the joy rush out of her body so quickly.

She felt the same now.

A dark stab of fear penetrated her heart. Was it *her* fear? Was *she* afraid? Or was she just reacting to the fear she saw in their eyes? It didn't matter. If she could feel the fear, it was also *her* fear. Not yet ready to fully accept this understanding, she said, "I'm fine. I realized something and it seemed...amusing. No big deal. Really, everything is okay."

Susan was afraid to say more, afraid they would think she was crazy. Oh God, *was* she? Is this what it felt like to have a nervous breakdown? One of the first signs of a breakdown was the inability to control your feelings, wasn't it? And to laugh at things others didn't think were humorous? And isn't that what she was doing? Oh please, God, I don't want to be crazy. "Everything's fine. It just seemed...funny," she repeated, wishing she could find some way to divert the attention away from her.

"Wait, Suze," Vicki persisted, "you *saw* something. I was watching you. You saw something. It looked like fun. Tell us. I'd sure like to know."

Susan felt Vicki's sincerity, and she wanted to hug her. But she also wanted to hide. It was her old fear returning, her fear of upsetting people with the clarity of her vision — her fear of telling them the *truth*. It was the same fear she and Saint Germain had discussed.

She remembered her vow *not* to hide. Maybe now was a perfect time to honor her promise to be open and vulnerable. After all, she was among friends, people who loved her. They just didn't understand. Well, so what, *she* didn't understand everything, either. That made them equal.

"Yes, I saw something, but I don't understand how to explain it, except that we can lighten up about what's been going on, even the earthquake. It's part of a plan, and it's the way it needs to be. It struck me as amusing because...oh, I don't know...just because," she replied, throwing her hands up in the air.

"Are you saying we shouldn't take this seriously?" Jeff asked.

"Well, I..."

Jeff didn't give her a chance to finish. "*You* take it seriously. You glue yourself to that TV over there, and you seem to get pretty worked up over what's happening."

Susan's first impulse was to deny this truth, but she didn't. "Yes, I do," she replied, sighing. "I guess it's what I need to do." Gazing into their expectant faces, she added,

"Look, I'm not saying that we shouldn't pay attention to all of this, but it's..." She paused, searching for the best words. "It's a *learning* experience. It's not really life and death. We can lighten up about it."

Vicki leaned forward in her chair, obviously interested. "A learning experience about what?"

"About life. About *us*. About the fact that we're all in this together...even people like President Storr who *look* like they're on the other side. We're all One, but we've forgotten it. Oh hell, guys, that's all I understand now."

Glenn laughed derisively. "Personally, I still think you flipped out."

Susan stifled her impulse to defend herself, to say something smart in return. "I can understand that. It must seem pretty weird what I did. It even bothers *me* a little." Susan stopped and read his energy: He was *very* uncomfortable. She must have said something to trigger his discomfort. It took but a second for her to understand, and she responded to this: "When I said that we're taking it too seriously, I wasn't saying anything *bad* about you. I mean, I wasn't criticizing you or laughing at you."

Glenn relaxed a little. "Okay. Not flipped out...but you're definitely way out there someplace."

"I agree, way out there is probably accurate. Or maybe it's more like way *in*."

Still not satisfied, Jeff persisted, "Hon, if you weren't laughing at us, what *were* you laughing at?"

Susan shrugged her shoulders. "It's like a big cosmic joke. Don't you ever feel like laughing at life even though you don't exactly know why?"

"Oh sure," Jeff answered, relieved to find something he could comfortably relate to.

Vicki took Susan's hand. "But it was more than that, wasn't it?"

Susan nodded.

"Promise you'll share it with us when you get it figured out. Promise?"

Susan nodded, her eyes filling with tears. She cried softly for a few minutes. Vicki handed her some tissue. Jeff came over and sat next to her. Then, little by little, they resumed their conversation. They even made popcorn.

Already the intensity of Susan's inner experience was fading. The clarity of a few minutes ago was now dimming, and she had the horrible thought that she would forget the beautiful truths she had learned.

No, she said to herself. I intend to remember what I need to remember, and what I need to remember is that it's a *game*. It's a game filled with illusions. The illusions can confuse me if I let them, so I intend to remain clear about what is truth and what is illusion.

I also intend to remember that Earth is a school, and that I came to this Earth-School to learn many things. The object is *to learn what I came here to learn and to enjoy myself along the way.*

That's all I have to remember now.

Having reminded herself of these truths, her fear vanished.

Chapter Fifteen
The Mark of the Beast

Revelations: 13:16: And he causeth all, both small and great, rich and poor, free and bond, to receive a mark in their right hand, or in their foreheads:

Revelations: 13:17: And that no man might buy or sell, save he that had the mark, or the name of the beast, or the number of his name.

=====

With all the tragedies that had recently befallen their country, the American people hungered for news, especially news of the California earthquake. It was no surprise, therefore, that the President's Wednesday news conference drew the largest audience in television history, surpassing even that of the 1996 Super Bowl.

Vicki and Glenn had stayed in Mount Shasta to continue house hunting, and they joined Susan and Jeff to watch President Storr's speech.

Susan's feelings about the President had changed. While she didn't exactly *like* him, she did feel more neutral towards him now. He was, after all, a player in the Cosmic Game, and, like everyone else, he was doing what he needed to do. She wondered if *he* knew he was a player? Probably not.

Still, something about President Storr bothered her. There was something *different* about him. What was it? Watching him intently as he prepared to speak, she asked for the understanding, but it eluded her.

As usual, the President appeared stiff and ill at ease. "My fellow Americans," he began, "the events of the past few days have shocked and saddened every one of us, and our thoughts and our prayers go out to those in California who have suffered so much. However, it is now time to put our grief behind us. It is time for *action*. We must begin the rebuilding of California. We must rebuild homes and businesses. We must put shattered lives back together. We must give the people in California a sense of hope...especially the children, for the children are the future of this great land of ours.

"As I indicated on Monday, we do not have the resources to meet this great crisis. We cannot do it by ourselves. We need help, and help is now forthcoming." The President paused, shuffling through his papers, searching for something.

Susan peered hard at the flickering image on the television screen. "There is something *odd* about him."

"Like what?" Glenn asked.

"Something odd. He's so *stiff*. Does he look real to you?"

Startled, Jeff asked, "Real? You mean real as in "real person"? It's a joke, right?"

Susan slid over next to him, put her arm around him, and tickled him. "Unh-unh, I wouldn't kid you, would I?"

"Oh sure," he replied, gently squeezing her arm. "You want me to seriously consider that the President of the United States might not be real? Next thing you'll tell me is that there are people living inside the moon. There aren't, are there?"

"Mm. I have some thoughts about that actually," Susan answered playfully. "I'd like to tell you about Mars, too. Interesting place. Seems that..."

"Sh!" Glenn demanded. "Can we debate this great issue later? I want to hear what he has to say."

Finding the paper he was looking for, the President resumed, "On Monday, I told you of a very generous offer by certain international agencies. It is my pleasure to announce to you that after careful deliberation we have decided to accept this offer of financial assistance.

"Now, my friends, it is not my purpose to hide the truth from you. The amount we need to borrow is enormous, in the trillions of dollars. Believe me, we searched for other ways to finance the reconstruction costs. This loan is the only way to help the earthquake victims in California."

The President leaned forward and smiled broadly. "Now, let us be realistic for a moment. The amount we are requesting *is* large, and these agencies naturally have a few requests of us. It is the same as if you or I requested a loan from our neighborhood bank—our banker would want us to meet certain conditions. It is the same with these international agencies.

"First, they have proposed, and we have agreed, that some of this rebuilding money should come from the American people themselves. Therefore, at this time I am announcing a 10 percent National Sales Tax to run for a period of at least one year. I realize this will be a sacrifice for you, but I am also sure that, with some reflection, you will see the necessity for it."

Glenn shook his head in disbelief. "Wow, that will do the economy in for sure."

"Why?" Vicki asked.

"Wait. I want to hear this!" Glenn demanded.

The President continued, "The second request is perhaps more difficult to understand, although we are sure that once the situation is fully explained to you, you will see the wisdom in the changes we are proposing." He took a deep breath. "The international lending agencies, along with our own Federal Reserve and the major banking institutions in this country, have decided that a restructuring of our currency is in order. They propose, first, the calling in of all outstanding currency."

Gasps of disbelief from the stunned audience temporarily interrupted the President.

Glenn shared their shock. "No! No way! He can't do that! Everything will come apart if he does that! The man's totally crazy!"

Holding up his hand for quiet, the President resumed, "I want to assure you that there will be absolutely no devaluation of the money you now have. It will retain it's full value. So please, have no fears about that.

"Let me explain why we are calling in the currency. We have an outdated and a clumsy currency system. It worked for our grandfathers, but it does *not* work for us. It impedes the efficient flow of business. It is outdated and it is *costly*. It is time for us to move into the modern age. It is time for us to institute a new monetary policy."

The President gripped the podium with both hands. "We propose replacing the old currency system with something new and modern—we call it the National Debit Card System. Perhaps some of you are familiar with the concept of the debit card. It will work much like the credit cards you now use, except that there will be only one card—the debit card—instead of the hundreds now in circulation.

"This one card system, this new cashless way of doing business, will save us an enormous amount of money. The Federal Reserve Research Council estimates we will save billions of dollars. These are dollars that we now spend in the processing of paper checks, in the handling of credit card accounts, and in the printing and handling of our paper currency. We can no longer afford to waste these dollars. They are needed—*desperately* needed—to help rebuild this wounded country."

Glenn chuckled. "The Fed got what it wanted. They've wanted this debit card for years. They're smart. They waited for exactly the right time to push for it. They know Washington is on the ropes. They have them exactly where they want them."

By now, reporters and other media people were milling around the room. Many had gathered in little groups, talking excitedly among themselves. The near pandemonium did not seem to bother the President. "The other benefit is the elimination of the drug trade. The drug lords and the pushers *depend* on currency; they *must* have it to carry on their evil trafficking. Without currency, they will be out of business!" he shouted, banging his fist on the podium.

The television camera moved in close. "We know that these ideas are new and startling to most of you, and that it may take you awhile to feel comfortable with them. Some of you may resist. You may feel that we are taking away a freedom. Believe me, that is not our intent. Our intent is to modernize our way of doing business. We live in the computer age, and this is a golden opportunity to take full advantage of the new computer technologies. Thanks to these advances, we can have a very logical monetary system in this country...logical and *efficient*.

"Okay, how will the debit card work? We have created a new Cabinet level agency called the Debit Card Board. This agency will be responsible for the day-to-day operation of the debit card. First, they will give each of you a number. For most of you this will be your existing Social Security number. If you are one of the few who do not have a Social Security card, the Board will assign you a number. Then they will open a debit card account for you using your number. The rest is pretty simple: The money you earn on your job goes directly into your account; the same for any money you receive from entitlement programs such as Social Security.

"Then, when you wish to buy something or pay a bill or pay your taxes, you use your number, and the computer deducts the money from your debit card account. It's automatic. No checks to write, no letters to mail, no costly trips to the bank. The computer will handle all transactions. The savings in time and in labor will be tremendous."

"These changes will, of course, take congressional approval. I must emphasize that we are working on a tight time frame. The lending agencies have given us a scant two weeks to debate these issues and then to pass the required legislation. I am therefore instructing both houses of Congress to clear their agendas and to begin work on these measures immediately.

"These are grave times, my friends. We must act swiftly and with determination."

The President stopped, his face darkening with suppressed anger. "Now, I must address something I find extremely disturbing. I have recently been accused of not being willing to respond to your questions. This isn't true. I would like nothing more than to sit and chat with you, but the pace of events does not allow this. There is no *time* for relaxed conversation. Much needs to be done. Nevertheless, I'll take a few questions now; but please, please try to *limit* them."

Glenn smiled ruefully. "Ever see a nation bought and sold before? Now you have. We've just been sold to the bankers—and most of them aren't even in this country."

Chapter Sixteen
More About the Beast

Revelations: 13:18: Here is wisdom. Let him that hath understanding count the number of the beast: for it is the number of a man; and his number is Six hundred threescore and six.

Although it was obvious that the President had concluded his remarks and that the time for questions was at hand, most of the media people continued to mill around.

President Storr waited. He tapped his fingers on the podium, his eyes flashing with impatience. "We need some order here. If you will please sit down, we can begin the questioning."

One by one the media representatives returned to their seats; but a full minute elapsed before the commotion subsided and Harry Stapleton from United News Service raised his hand.

The President nodded at him. "Yes, over in the corner, Mr. Stapleton."

"Mr. President, doesn't this new policy amount to a complete takeover of our monetary system by outsiders?"

"No, certainly not. It is simply a logical extension of the system we already have. How many credit cards do *you* have, Mr. Stapleton?"

"Oh, I don't know…six or seven I guess."

"Do you transact most of your business with these cards?"

"Well yes, I suppose so, but what does that have to do with my question?"

"We are simply suggesting an extension of the system that is already in place. It's a simpler and more cost effective version of that system."

"Mr. President, that still doesn't answer the question. Who exactly will be in charge of these new debit cards?"

The President's irritation was obvious. "As I said before, the Debit Card Board will be in charge of implementing and overseeing this new system."

"Am I correct in assuming that the Fed will control the Debit Card Board?"

"The Fed will certainly play a major role; but the Board will also have representatives from the major US banks, along with other members of the business community…and the federal government of course. We will be there to safeguard the interests of the citizens of this country."

"Do you truly feel they need safeguarding, Mr. President?" another reporter inquired slyly.

"Ah…no, that was simply a figure of speech."

Harry Stapleton had one more question, "The International Monetary Fund and the World Bank and the other international lending agencies you spoke of, how much control will *they* have over the Debit Card Board?"

President Storr hesitated, and it was obvious to everyone in the room that he did not want to respond to this question. "They may have some small advisory role. That is all we envision at this time."

"A small advisory role?"

"Yes."

"But, sir, this is precisely what worries me, and this is what prompted my original question. Who *are* these international agencies? And how can we be sure they will act in the best interests of the United States? And who is to say they will not usurp more and more power over this new board?"

"We do not anticipate that they will have more than a token voice in the day-to-day operations of the Debit Card Board."

"Can you give us any more solid assurance than that?"

"I do not feel I need to."

The two men glared at each other. Harry Stapleton glanced down at the floor, shaking his head, obviously unhappy with the President's reply. But he did not pursue his question.

Another reporter asked, "Sir, are you saying that there will be no cash whatsoever once the debit card is introduced?"

"That is correct. Why would there be? There is no need for it," the President replied curtly.

"What about the smaller banks and the credit unions? What will happen to them?"

"My understanding is that some of them will have a role to play. Some. Although, to be honest, most will be phased out." The President shrugged his shoulders. "These institutions are too small. We must organize our banking system into larger units if we are to be efficient. Of course, those people who lose their jobs will receive retraining and job placement assistance."

A well-known network anchorman asked the question that would trouble many in the coming days, "What if someone doesn't want to be a part of this new plan?"

The President leaned forward, resting his arms casually on the podium. "No one will be coerced. We are not in the business of forcing anyone to do something they don't want to do."

The distinguished looking, silver-haired anchorman persisted. "Mr. President, let's be realistic. With no cash, won't everyone *have* to be a part of this plan? How would they live if they didn't have the card?"

The President visibly tensed. "It is not our intent to coerce *anyone*."

"But they'll *have* to take this card, won't they?" another puzzled reporter asked. "How would they avoid it?"

The President's eyes narrowed, and when he spoke the

anger radiated out from him in almost palpable waves. "It is time for this great country to come together. We have suffered grievous wounds, and we must heal them. Sometimes the healing process takes extraordinary measures, and sometimes it is easy to misunderstand the intent of these measures. It is easy to jump to the wrong conclusions. You must be patient. Do not judge us so quickly. Give us time." He forced himself to smile. "These are good questions you have asked. Congress will debate these same questions...and many others in the next few days. That is the job of your elected representatives, is it not? All points of view will be heard in the Congressional debates I assure you." He glanced at his watch. "In less than 10 minutes, I am to meet with the majority leaders of both Houses to discuss the very issues you have raised."

"The country will never recover," Glenn said quietly.

Vicki appeared confused. "I still don't get it. What's the point of calling in the currency?"

"He said it's to save money," Jeff answered.

Glenn shook his head. "Unh-unh, I don't buy that. Sure, it would save *some* money, but I don't think that's the true reason."

"So what's the *real* reason?" Jeff asked.

"It's the big boys playing their money game. There have been hints of this for a long time, rumors of a secret organization that makes most of the world's decisions. I think we're seeing them in action now."

"A group more powerful than the federal government?"

"Lots more powerful."

"Powerful enough to control Washington?"

"Hard to say. You have to understand how money—big money—works in this world. I wouldn't say the money boys exactly *dictate* to Washington...although if they can force the Feds to call in the currency and to issue a debit card, then I'd say they're pretty much in control."

They silently pondered what Glenn had just said.

"Taylor Caldwell wrote about these things in some of her novels, didn't she?" Susan asked. "I remember her talking about a secret world government in one or two of her books."

Glenn nodded. "I've read a couple of them. Pretty perceptive stuff. Other people have written about it, too."

"Glenn, how does this new debit card work?" Jeff asked.

"It's not exactly a new idea," Glenn answered. "In fact, they proposed a version of the debit card a few years ago in Australia. The Aussies didn't like it and they voted it down. Smart move if you want *my* opinion. We get some feelers here in this country every once in awhile. Nothing solid— just some trial balloons to see how the public would take to such an idea. I guess the money guys didn't think it would fly, because they didn't push it...until now."

Vicki appeared impatient with Glenn's answer. "But what *is* it, hon?"

"Like Storr says, it's a national credit card. It's the cashless society people have been talking about for years. You'll get a number, and you'll have to use it if you want to make any transactions."

Jeff leaned forward in his chair and asked, "You wouldn't be able to buy *anything* without a number. Right? Groceries, gas, stuff like that?"

"That's the theory. The way I've heard it described, they'll link all the cash registers to computers—like they do now in some of the shopping malls. That's pretty commonplace these days. The difference is in this new system they'll hook the smaller computers up to one or two super computers." Glenn shrugged his shoulders. "What can I tell you. That's the way we'll do business in this country. No cash, no checks, no credit. You punch in your number and the computers take over. That's the program. You wouldn't have much choice."

"Unless you did things another way," Susan countered.

Glenn raised his eyebrows. "What do you mean?"

"Maybe we have to change some of our attitudes," Susan argued. "Maybe we've gotten hooked on money, addicted to how easy it is. Like we did with the credit cards when they first came out. Maybe it's time to make some changes. You don't *have* to use money, do you? You could use barter. I imagine lots of people use barter and trade."

Jeff seemed skeptical. "Not anymore."

"I bet they do in the country...like back in the hills."

"Yeah, you're probably right, but..."

Glenn nodded. "Or you could use something else for money, like gold or silver or sea shells, or whatever everyone agreed was valuable," he said. "So you're right, there would be ways around it. Not for most people, though. They'll accept the new system. They might grumble a bit, but they'll accept it. Storr's right; for most people it's an extension of the credit card system they already use. It's really just a super credit card—a *national* credit card. They'll go for it...if it's merchandised right."

Jeff made a face and shook his head. "This could be scary. For instance, let's say there's no more cash, just this debit card. Let's also say you don't have any gold or silver or conch shells, or anything else of value. Now, what if you want to move to another city or another state, and someone doesn't want you to move? If they had access to the super computers, it would be easy to prevent you from moving, wouldn't it? All they'd have to do is program the computers to deny you the use of your card in the other locality."

"I think I see where you're going," Glenn said.

"Yeah, and without the use of your card you couldn't move, even if you *wanted* to. I guess you could move, but you couldn't *buy* anything once you got there. You couldn't support yourself. You couldn't survive."

"Another thing, wouldn't they know everything about you?" Vicki asked. "With everything you buy being fed into some super computer, they'd know everything. Right down to the kind of toothpaste you prefer."

Susan chuckled. "It's going to be interesting, folks."

Jeff looked surprised. "You sound like you're looking forward to this."

Susan thought a moment. "Yes, I think I am. I've been listening to you talk. You're right, there's a hidden agenda in what Storr is proposing, and it has to do with controlling people's lives. That part bothers me a bit. It could bother

me a *lot* if I dwelled on it. I could get worried how we're
going to survive in this new system...and how we're going
to keep our freedom." Susan got up and walked slowly
around the room. She absentmindedly picked up a small
wooden duck from the coffee table, running her fingers
over its smooth green back. "I'm not going to do that,
though. The way I see it there's another side to this. It's an
opportunity to grow, to see how resourceful we are, to see
how *creative* we are. Does that sound corny?" she asked.
She didn't give anyone a chance to reply. "It doesn't matter, it works for me," she continued, more to herself than to
anyone else. She turned the small green duck over in her
hand, then gently replaced it on the table. "Anyway, I guess
what I'm saying is, I've changed my point of view about
what's happening; now it feels like I'm on an adventure. It
all depends on our pictures of reality—you know, those
pictures we all carry around in our head that define life for
us. Personally, my picture is that I'm on an adventure."

Jeff gazed at her as if he was seeing a stranger. He
smiled ruefully. "You used to be so practical. You used to
think everything out so carefully. You used to worry for
both of us. Now...now you seem like some teenager out on
a lark."

"I like that picture," Susan exclaimed happily. "I didn't
have much fun as a teenager the first time around. Maybe
I'll give myself a chance to do it again."

"That's fine, but..." Jeff began.

Before he could finish his thought, Susan walked behind him and rubbed his shoulders.

"Hey, you know I can't think when you do that," he
protested.

"I understand completely," Susan said as she tousled
his hair. "That's the point—time to give the old brain a
breather." She rested her hands on his head. "Our brains
always take things so seriously, don't you think? Always
worrying and fretting. Always seeing problems. Always
thinking everything has to do with survival. It gets boring...and so...*heavy*. I want a new way to look at life, so
I've decided to turn my brain off for awhile and to have a

sense of humor about everything that's happening. *That's* the practical approach. You'll see."

Chapter Seventeen
Friends Gather Together

From *Endtimes*: "In the late eighties and
the early nineties, those extraterrestrial
masters who had incarnated on the Planet
to co-create a "Heaven on Earth" began
slowly—very slowly—to awaken to their
true identity.

Then, they searched each other out
and gathered together...for it was time.

They called themselves the "Family of
Light."

At first the Forces of Darkness took
little notice of this gathering, for although possessed of much wisdom, the
Forces of Darkness do not really understand the Forces of Light, and they usually underestimate them."

The Congress of the United States was about to decide
the fate of the Debit Card Proposal, and for the next ten
days most of the country glued themselves to C-Span as the
House and the Senate debated this issue. The Halls of
Congress rang with many impassioned pleas both for and
against the "Card." To most viewers, it seemed a toss-up
which side would prevail. But, after the last speech was

finished and the last vote counted, Congress voted down the President's proposal—there would be no debit card. The nation still had her currency, but also trillions of dollars in quake related cleanup and reconstruction costs—and no funds to pay for them.

Later that evening, in a terse one-sentence statement, the consortium of international bankers withdrew its offer of a loan.

The White House had no comment.

Dawn of the next day saw the end of the storm in California, and the long-range forecast was for an extended period of clearing. The good weather was too late, however, for the damage was already done.

The California quake, the mightiest in recorded history, continued to send shock waves rippling through the length and breadth of the land. In California, the state's two largest insurers declared that they could not possibly honor the avalanche of claims that were pouring in. Bankruptcy, they declared, was their only alternative. They reminded Washington of its promise to help, but Washington was quick to respond that without the loan from the international bankers they had no money for a bailout of the insurance companies.

Meanwhile, the bill for the cleanup in California mounted—with no one able to pay for it.

Hearing this depressing news, an already nervous Wall Street panicked. Two days after Congress defeated the Debit Card Proposal, the Market lost 900 points, the greatest one day loss in its history. Although up 125 points the next day, it lost another 600 points the following day and almost the same amount the day after that. In four days, the Market had lost one third of its value.

To avoid a total collapse of the Market, President Storr halted trading on the New York Stock Exchange. An angry President blamed Congress for the Market's precipitous slide, calling their defeat of the Debit Card Bill shortsighted and "The worst kind of partisan politics." He warned of further serious consequences if Congress did not reconsider its vote.

The media, too, blamed the Congress for the nation's woes. The country's most influential dailies called for the impeachment of any member of Congress who had voted against the passage of the Debit Card Bill.

At the same time, in an extensive and rare front-page interview, the Chairman of the Federal Reserve declared that his agency had done its best—it had no more tricks up its sleeve. In his opinion, the only hope for economic recovery lay in the restructuring of the nation's currency system and in a massive infusion of new money into the nation's economy. On these issues, it seemed, the Chairman and the President were in full agreement.

Wall Street was not the only sector of the economy to panic. Worried depositors, anxiously eyeing the Market's near collapse, nervously lined up to withdraw their savings from banks all across the country. Two of New York City's largest banks, and one in Boston, their cash reserves nearly depleted, closed their doors to avoid a total panic. Sensing a coming disaster unless he acted quickly, President Storr shut down the nation's banking system, declaring the next two days to be official "bank holidays."

To even the most optimistic observer, the nation's economy seemed to teeter on the verge of collapse.

Although far from New York, the mood in Mount Shasta, and other small cities and towns across the country, was one of nervous anticipation as people suddenly realized that the country might be in very serious trouble.

It was in this atmosphere that Evelyn called her circle of friends, announcing that Saint Germain desired to talk with them through his channel, Veda.

However, instead of the eight or nine who usually attended Veda's channelings, by 7:30 more than fifty worried Mount Shasta residents had packed themselves into every corner of Evelyn's living room, eager to hear what Saint Germain would have to say about the nation's crisis.

Perhaps because of the larger number of people, or because of the high level of anxiety most of them felt, there was much milling around and changing of seats. Veda waited patiently for a few minutes, then asked, "Can everyone hear me? Can you hear me in the back?"

"Fine! Loud and clear!" someone yelled.

Veda nodded, folded her hands in her lap, and surveyed the audience. "My goodness, there certainly are lots of people tonight. I've never channeled for so many people before...but I guess there's always a first time," she said, laughing nervously. "I can feel the energy in the room. It's pretty intense. Sometimes it's hard to bring Saint Germain in with the energy level so high. Could you all relax a little? Maybe you could take a few deep breaths." She waited while the audience followed her advice. "Okay, that's much better. Thanks. Now, if you will close your eyes and go within we will welcome Saint Germain."

Veda closed her own eyes and breathed deeply. "Greetings, beloved ones," Saint Germain murmured softly and tenderly. "And how is everyone this evening?"

Two people replied "good," but without much enthusiasm. The rest were silent.

"There is much to discuss tonight. Much indeed. The events that are taking place are having a profound effect on you, are they not?"

A smattering of nervous laughter greeted Saint Germain's question.

"Indeed. Your world suddenly seems turned upside down, does it not? This confuses you, so many of you look to your leaders for direction; and yet your leaders do not...Mm...they do not seem to be at home. So you wonder just who is minding the store."

An explosive outburst of laughter greeted *this* remark. It was a full minute before Saint Germain could continue.

"Your laughter says much, beloved ones, for it speaks of the uncertainty and the fear within you. You fear *all* the walls may come tumbling down, do you not?"

"Yes!" many answered in unison.

"Indeed, and would this be such a bad thing?"

Silence greeted Saint Germain's question. Then Anna spoke. "It feels like it. So many have died recently, and now it feels like...like everything is coming apart. What are we supposed to do?" she asked, the helplessness evident in her voice.

Saint Germain took a moment to respond. "Indeed, many have left your Planet, and many more will leave before long. And do you mourn those who have left their embodiment?"

A tear rolled slowly down Anna's cheek. Gently brushing it away with her hand, she answered, "Well...yes."

"Do you not know, beloved one, that for each being this was a choice made deep within the soul, and that this choice is a further step on their evolutionary path?"

"I suppose so. At least I understand it up here," Anna replied, pointing to her head. "But my heart grieves for all my brothers and sisters who still suffer...especially the children."

Saint Germain paused, choosing his words carefully. "There is a reason for all of this," he said softly. "For the chaos and the suffering. The old must crumble before the new can arise." He paused again. "The new *is* arising you know." Pausing yet a third time, he gazed out over the subdued audience, an enigmatic smile on his face. All was quiet in the room. "Is this not what you have dreamed of? And come to this Planet to help create? And worked so hard for?"

"But does it have to happen like this?" someone from the back of the room asked. It was Karen, whose brother was still missing and presumed to have perished.

"Of course not. Nothing is predetermined. There are always many possibilities. Yet this is the path you have chosen." Saint Germain paused. "You *do* know that you have chosen this path, do you not?" A long silence followed. Someone coughed. "Well, you *have*, along with many of your brothers and sisters."

The man sitting next to Susan asked, "Saint Germain, what's the *purpose* of this?"

"These recent events represent a coming together—a *clash*—of energies in your country. Great energies indeed. There is a divine purpose in this. It is a great healing and a wondrous cleansing."

Although she felt intimidated by the large number of people, many of whom she did not know, Susan asked a question, "Saint Germain, you have a different perspective. You see the bigger picture. What do *you* see happening…you know…in the near future?"

Instead of answering her question directly, Saint Germain chose his own way of responding. "Ah, Blessed One, and how is it that you are this evening?"

Startled by Saint Germain's reply, she could not answer. Instead, her focus narrowed, and for a moment it was as if she and Saint Germain were the only two in the room. It seemed to her that they were old, old friends who had re-united after a long separation, and that they were about to bring each other up to date on their comings and goings.

"You have understood much in the past few days, have you not, beloved one?"

Still unable to speak, Susan simply nodded.

"And is this not a wondrous event?"

Something in Saint Germain's tone or in the vibration of his speech was so *personal*—so loving and warm and personal—that his words went to the very center of her, to her heart.

Saint Germain did not hurry her, nor did anyone else in the room. She traveled deep within herself, into her opened heart. *Then she was inside her own heart, Saint Germain standing beside her.* A beautiful violet light surrounded them. It *bathed* them. The light was healing and loving — the light was *alive*.

Time stopped for Susan. She was in the eternal Now Moment.

Then she "returned" to the room, aware of the chair she was sitting in, of Jeff beside her, and of the other people in the audience. She had no idea how long she had been gone, nor did she care. She glanced at Saint Germain, and the love in his eyes reminded her of what had just happened. She cried, then smiled through her tears, for they were tears of joy.

"Give me a minute, my friend," she said softly.

"Of course, beloved one."

Someone handed her a box of tissues. Susan blew her nose and took a deep breath, ready to ask her question of Saint Germain. Only it was not the question she had first intended.

Chapter Eighteen
Truth

From *Endtimes*: "As we have said, there were those who dreamed of controlling the Earth. To do this, they needed to define reality for the masses...which meant that they needed to restrict the free flow of information. Taking the most direct route, they simply bought the media, then systematically undermined, vilified, and scorned anyone who contradicted the "official line."

Those in the New Age movement came under attack very quickly. The media portrayed them as Satanists and kooks, born-again hippies, and airy-fairy weirdoes.

The tactic worked—for awhile. The general population "learned" to mistrust the New Age Community, and they rejected the wisdom this group had brought to the Planet.

But not even the Dark Forces could stem the flow of this precious Truth for long."

Susan gazed into Saint Germain's knowing eyes. "Saint

Germain, something wonderful just happened inside me. I'm not sure how to describe it. Can you help me find the words?"

"It was a grand merging of heart energy."

"Yes, it *was* in my heart. Did we both create it?"

"Of course."

"Because we both *wanted* it?"

"Indeed."

Susan quietly considered this for a moment. It was an almost overwhelming thought to realize that Saint Germain was inside her open heart, and that on some level their heart energies had *merged*.

The room was quiet. Then a chair squeaked as someone shifted around in their seat. Susan nodded. "This gives me much to ponder. I think I'll go within and ask for more understanding. There was something else I was going to ask. Is that okay?"

"Of course."

"It has to do with the changes and the destruction happening on the Earth. In my vision, I see this upheaval continuing for quite some time. There's a darkness on the land. Not everywhere, though, and *that's* the part I don't understand."

"You will."

"Okay. I'll wait for that understanding, then." She was quiet for a moment. "I also see many beings on the Planet who would take our power if we let them. I'm not sure who they are, only that they have planned much of what has recently happened. Like the assassination of President Tipton. It *was* planned by these beings, wasn't it?"

"Indeed."

"I also see much fear in the country. This fear is like a disease. It weakens people. It makes them susceptible to being manipulated. Could you tell me more about this?"

"Recall your vision, beloved one."

Susan closed her eyes and went within. "Oh. I see. People are afraid there won't be enough food and other basic necessities. They are afraid they won't *survive*. They begin to panic. It's like they're drowning, and they'll do almost anything to keep from going under. They will listen to *any-one* who promises to save them, even if it means giving their power away. And there are many beings who would take their power, aren't there?"

"Indeed."

"Is this going to happen?"

"For some."

"For those of us in the room?"

"Possibly...for some of you. Each will make a choice."

"For me?"

"What do *you* think?"

"I feel everything is okay. I feel protected." She hesitated, reluctant to say what she was thinking, afraid that even Saint Germain would judge her. When she spoke, her voice was so low that many in the room had to lean forward to hear her words. "Sometimes I feel almost exhilarated when I think of what is to come. I don't understand this feeling. I don't want anyone to suffer, and yet...and yet it seems almost *exciting* that everything is moving so quickly and that the old forms are crumbling. I don't like to admit this. I don't like to admit how excited I am, because I'm afraid that others will misunderstand."

"Mm, they *might*...if they see these changes as negative or as a threat to their well-being. Some may choose to interpret events in this way, of course, and because of this attitude may see you as...Mm...somewhat ghoulish. They may judge you as someone who enjoys the suffering of others."

"Yes, that's it, that's what bothers me."

"Indeed, beloved one. Yet it is not your intention that others suffer. You do not enjoy this, do you?"

"No."

"Your wish is for a grand love to be on this Planet...as it has in time's past."

"Yes."

"You have expanded your *consciousness*, that is all. You are a way-shower. You have a *vision*. And you expect that others will share your vision, do you not?"

"Yes."

"Understand, beloved one, that those of your brothers and sisters who live in fear and in grand separation of self may reject your vision; and when they reject your *vision*, they will *seem* to be rejecting *you*. This is not the truth. It is *themselves* they reject. It is of no cause for concern."

"I know you're right, but it still bothers me."

"What is it *precisely* that bothers you?"

"That others will think I am odd for feeling excited by the changes and the destruction."

"Why is it you care what others think?" Saint Germain inquired in a lighthearted, almost teasing way.

Susan shrugged her shoulders, feeling slightly annoyed at his question. "I don't know."

"What is your opinion of *yourself* for having these feelings of excitement?"

Susan grinned sheepishly. "Oh, sure, I get it—it's *me* I'm disapproving of. I'm just using the others as a projection screen for my own feelings of self criticism."

"Precisely."

"That's a hard one to get sometimes."

"It is the Divine Mirror. Sometimes the Mirror reflects back that which you are not yet ready to see, that is all."

Susan sighed. "That's for sure. And it's always the aspects of me that I most need to see that I avoid looking at."

"It will become easier. It takes practice. Is there more you wish to know?"

"I want to know about Jeff. How will he make it through these coming times?"

"Perhaps it is *he* who needs to ask this question," Saint Germain gently reminded her.

Susan leaned her head close to Jeff and whispered, "Do you want to ask anything about yourself?"

Looking very much on the spot, Jeff shifted around in his seat. Then, clearing his throat, he said, "I guess so; except I'm not sure what to say."

Saint Germain's steady gaze measured Jeff for a few seconds. "What is it you fear, beloved one?"

Jeff didn't hesitate. "I'm afraid everything is totally coming apart."

"Indeed it is. And is there more you fear?"

"I'm afraid I won't be able to take care of Susan."

"This woman you are with, do you think she needs protecting?"

"Sure. I'm her husband. That's my job, isn't it?" Jeff answered defensively.

Someone in the back of the room giggled. Saint Germain took no notice. "And is this not felt as a burden?"

"Sometimes," Jeff sighed.

"Yet you cling to it. Why is that?"

"I guess I'm afraid I'd *lose* her if I didn't take care of her."

"Beloved Master, you and this wondrous woman are joined for all eternity. You could not lose this connection even if you wished to. You have been together many times you know."

"We have? Oh, you mean in other lifetimes." Jeff laughed, still not believing in this phenomenon.

"Indeed."

"I don't understand very much about that."

"Indeed, beloved one. She can assist you to remember...if you desire this."

"I'm not sure. I guess I need to think about it."

"You have been her wife in another lifetime. Did you know this?"

"Her *wife*?"

"Indeed."

"Hm. Now that *would* be interesting to remember. It would put a different light on things that are happening now." Mystified, he added, "I have no idea why I said that...but I'm sure it's true."

"You will be more in the understanding when you allow the remembrance of other incarnations."

"Okay, you've convinced me. I'll do it."

"Good. Is there more you wish to ask?"

"I guess not."

"Are we finished, then?"

"Yes. Thanks, I feel better."

"Thank *you*, beloved one."

Saint Germain glanced around the room, his dark, penetrating eyes absorbing everything. "Are there more questions?"

"Yes, Saint Germain, I have a question," Evelyn said. "You stated that President Tipton was assassinated. Could you say more about this?"

"This man who chose to be your leader had recently come into much understanding—much awareness—of the forces at work in this your country. He was contemplating sharing these understandings with his fellow countrymen. He felt it was his *duty* to do so."

"Are you saying he was killed because of this?"

"Indeed."

"Why?"

"His revelations would have changed the balance of power."

Evelyn considered this for a moment, then asked, "I've always believed that the CIA had something to do with President Kennedy's death. Did they also kill Tipton?"

"Mm...they had a part in this...as did many others. What this man was about to do threatened many. Many indeed."

"So, you're talking about a conspiracy?"

"That is one way to describe it. Let us say that there are many in your government and in your world of business who have their own plan—their own *dream*—for the future of this country...and for the world. These entities picked your President because he seemed to share these dreams. They considered him to be *safe*. For a time he *was*, but then he began to feel an intense guilt and remorse for having played the game and for having deceived you. He made up his mind, as you would say, to "spill the beans," and there were many in positions of power who decided that they could not allow him to do this."

"Who else is involved?"

"This will become clear shortly. Listen closely to those who would persuade you that they know what is best for you. Listen and trust *yourself* to know whether they indeed speak the truth for you."

It was Anna's turn to ask a question. "What about our new President, President Storr?"

"What is it you wish to know, beloved one?"

"Can we trust him?"

"Trusting another, you know, is often a way of relinquishing your power."

Anna shook her head. "I don't understand."

"When you trust another, does it not then become very important how they behave towards you? It does you know, for you now believe that your fate is in their hands. You have given away your power."

"I guess you're right," Anna agreed, smiling the smile of the innocent child. "You have lots of ways of warning us about the giving away of our power, don't you?"

"It is an understanding most of you have come to this Planet to learn."

"Boy, that's sure true for me. Mm…let's see…okay, let me put my question another way: Is President Storr also deceiving us the way President Tipton was? Is he playing the same game?"

"This man who was your second in command, and is now your leader, was picked very carefully. Very carefully indeed."

"You mean picked to be President?"

"Not exactly. He was carefully selected to be *second in command*, for there were those in your secret government who did not trust your President Tipton, and they wanted a reliable replacement for him should the need arise."

"When you say secret government, are you talking about the people who want to control us?"

"Indeed."

"Is Storr one of them?"

"He shares many of their dreams, yes."

Glenn raised his hand. "May I ask your opinion of the debit card?"

"It was this that your President Tipton was about to inform you of."

"You mean the truth about the card?"

"Indeed."

"What *is* the truth?"

"You are a keen observer of such matters, are you not, beloved one?"

"You could put it that way."

"Then you already have the answer to your own question...if you but search within and trust what you know."

Glenn seemed frustrated, but did not pursue the matter.

Saint Germain surveyed the room. "Are there more questions?" There was much stretching and moving about in the audience, but no questions. "Very well, then, I will say good-bye for now. But remember, although the road ahead may appear rocky, it is the path you have chosen. It need not be difficult, not really, not unless you *need* this experience. It is up to you. You are all Masters. I will bid you good evening for now."

Veda inhaled deeply and opened her eyes.

Chapter Nineteen
The Cashless Society

Revelations: 18:10: Standing afar off for fear of her torment, saying, Alas, alas, that great city Babylon, that mighty city! For in one hour is thy judgment come.

Revelations: 18:11: And the merchants of the Earth shall weep and mourn over her; for no man buyeth their merchandise anymore.

The country had been hit hard: a vital young President felled by an assassin's bullet; much of the State of California destroyed by the most violent earthquake in recorded history, with millions of lives lost and trillions of dollars in damage; and now the Stock Market panic that had pushed Wall Street to the edge of ruin.

To the average American it seemed the worst was over. It *had* to be.

Susan knew this not to be true, for her vision told her otherwise. For the moment, though, she did not share her understanding with others. Instead, she settled into her new home, taking long walks with Jeff and Sam, exploring the beautiful woods and creeks and meadows around Mount Shasta...and asking for guidance.

She asked for guidance because she knew that the country would soon be tested.

Most Americans did not share Susan's understanding, however. The believed—they *wanted* to believe—that the worst was over, that the "storm" had passed, and that better days lay just ahead. Thus, in spite of the recent turmoil and tragedy, a curious calm spread across the country, and for awhile all seemed well.

And the unfoldment of events in the next few days seemed to support this rising mood of optimism.

True, the defeat of the Debit Card Bill in Congress had prompted the international lending agencies to withdraw their offer of a loan; however, this did not precipitate the economic disaster many had predicted. True, the Market had lost much of its value, but Wall Street was showing signs of recovery. True, the situation in California had worsened; yet California seemed a long way off to most Americans, and the California quake seemed almost like a bad dream.

Life in most of the country, it seemed, was slowly returning to normal.

This was an illusion, however, an illusion that would soon be shattered by an event about to take place thousands of miles away.

The Japanese stock market—the Nikkei—had lost much of its value in the past few days. Nothing unusual about that; most of the world's markets had experienced similar losses. The Japanese government had stepped in, the losses had stopped, and the Nikkei had stabilized briefly. Then, for reasons that were never to be clear, the market collapsed. The panic selling began early in the morning. By late afternoon, the Japanese market simply ceased to exist. There were rumors of manipulation, of massive fraud, and of still more massive profit taking, but the stories were never proven.

The Nikkei collapse sent shock waves throughout the other world markets, shock waves as great and as devastating in their own way as those released by the California quake. One by one the other markets tumbled. The Market in the United States held out the longest—a valiant and almost unbelievable three days—but mighty as it was, it too succumbed.

Many in the United States, not understanding how the Market worked, believed that the crash was temporary, that the government—or *someone*—would do *something*, and that the Market would magically come back to life.

Glenn knew better. "There's nothing anyone can do. The Market's gone," he said wistfully. Although he had not been an active player on Wall Street for many years, he loved the excitement and the drama of the Market, and its passing saddened him.

Jeff looked skeptical. "Surely the government can pump some money in, can't they?"

Glenn shook his head. "No way. Look at the mess *they're* in. They don't have enough money to bail *anyone* out. Even if they did, it wouldn't work. The government can't just go out and buy stocks. The system doesn't oper-ate like that." Sipping his tea, he gazed up at Mount Shasta, lost in thought. "You see, the Market works because of in-vestor confidence, and right now there isn't any. It's zero. And I can see why. The crash has shown us the sickness in the economy. *I* wouldn't invest in it, and I can sure see why no one else wants to either. But hang on guys, it ain't over yet."

"You mean more problems?"

"You bet."

Glenn's prediction proved accurate. The day after the crash, the rumor quickly spread that the Federal Deposit In-surance Corporation—the agency responsible for insuring depositor's savings—was broke. If the FDIC was broke, then banks were not safe places to keep money. To a citi-zenry already nervous and jittery, or just downright scared, that's all it took to trigger the most massive bank panic in history.

By the next morning, people across the country had

lined up in front of banks, savings and loans, credit unions, and other financial institutions, demanding their money. When these besieged institutions ran out of funds, they closed their doors. There was nothing else they could do.

Washington urged calm and restraint as the only way to end the panic. The White House press releases claimed that the situation was not as bad as it seemed. "The banks will soon reopen and the economy will stabilize. Have faith — your country will not desert you," the President said. Few believed him.

People did not want to hear empty promises. They wanted their *money*. For years the FDIC had promised to reimburse any depositor who lost money because of a bank failure. Thousands of banks *had* failed, and millions of depositors now turned to the FDIC for help.

Although the FDIC was not as insolvent as the rumors claimed, it could do little to cope with a banking disaster of this magnitude. They reimbursed a scant 15 percent of depositors. Everyone else lost their money.

The collapse of the banking industry set a disastrous chain of events into motion: Frightened citizens clung to what little money they had, parting with it to buy absolute necessities and nothing more; which prompted businesses to cut back on inventory; which caused many factories to shut down; which caused more unemployment. Once started, this vicious cycle was impossible to stop.

The United States plunged into the worst depression in its history, much worse than the one following the crash of 1929. In a matter of days, most of the country's wealth ceased to exist. The first to disappear was "paper" wealth: stocks, bonds, securities, and most pension funds. This "money" vanished overnight.

President Storr made the obligatory appearance on national television to assure the country that the government had formulated a plan to bring a quick end to the economic disaster; but his words sounded oddly hollow, and in spite of the talk, nothing was done to ease the crisis.

Washington, it appeared, was paralyzed.

The reason for Washington's ineffectiveness soon became clear. The country had been bled dry. It had been bled dry by years of enormous interest payments on an out-of-control national debt, by "peace keeping" operations on many continents, and by an expensive arm's race that mysteriously dragged on despite the announced end to the Cold War. The result? There was no money available to pump into the economy: no money to rescue banks, no money to help restart downed businesses, and no money for unemployment payments.

For those who believed, or hoped, that the current crisis was only a nightmare—that the county would shake itself awake and get on with business—the following week brought bad news: more business failures, more plant closings, and more workers unemployed.

The impossible had happened—the United States of America, once the mightiest and richest nation on Earth, was broke.

Reactions were quick and varied. As in 1929, many individuals, unable to face what seemed to them to be a bleak and empty future, committed suicide. In the first three days of the crash, more than a hundred thousand people chose this path.

Although some social unrest had occurred during the earlier Great Depression, this time the unrest flared into an uncontrolled firestorm of violence. The cities suffered the most. Many urban dwellers, their lives almost unbelievably stressed by poverty, by persistent unemployment, and by soul-numbing racial discrimination, had lived on the edge of violence for years, and they snapped. Riots erupted in New York, Chicago, Detroit, Los Angeles, San Francisco and Las Vegas. Local and state authorities immediately declared martial law.

Most citizens reacted less violently. Theirs was a stunned, shocked silence. It was as if someone had just informed them that a cherished dream they had believed in all their lives would never come true. It was the American Dream of unending economic growth, of prosperity, and of financial independence. This dream had nourished them. It had kept them going. And now suddenly the dream had vanished—shattered by worldwide forces they did not understand.

They waited for some glimmer that things were not as bad as they knew them to be. It was all they could do.

Susan was quiet during these days of economic collapse. Quiet and pensive. She read the papers for awhile, then gave them up. The same with the television news programs. They wanted to divert attention from what was really happening, and she did not want her attention diverted. She wanted to know the truth.

She spent much time asking for guidance from within. When she wasn't meditating, she was walking the streets of Mount Shasta, watching the faces of the people, absorbing their energies, and reading the confusion and the fear and the pain in their hearts.

Most people did not understand what had happened. The old "realities," the old familiar forms, were crumbling quickly. What would replace these old forms? Would *anything* replace them? Something *had* to replace them—they gave meaning and structure to life. Without them...

Susan felt the pain and the confusion in those she passed on the streets, and she wanted to help. She knew her time of service would come...but not for awhile, for her vision told her that other events needed to unfold first.

In the meantime, she had other gifts to offer. She kept her sense of humor and her faith in the power of love. She knew that others received these gifts even if it was not on a conscious level.

While most Americans reacted to the economic collapse with a stunned lethargy, other powerful forces—secretive forces—made their move. For years they had dreamed of this opportunity. They had *longed* for it. It had come. The time to act was *now*.

On the eighth day after the Market crash, the consortium of international bankers repeated their offer. Only now it was more of a *demand* than an offer. They would

immediately pump two trillion dollars into the economy—
to restart downed businesses, to ensure everyone a job, and
to begin the reconstruction work in California. In exchange,
they demanded sweeping changes in the currency system.

These individuals understood the psyche of the average
American exceedingly well. Equally important, they
learned from their mistakes. They admitted to themselves
that they had pushed the debit card too fast. Most Americans were not psychologically prepared to switch to a cashless society so quickly—they were emotionally attached to
the idea of paper money, and they would first need to be
"weaned" away from this attachment.

With this in mind, the consortium decided to let Americans have their paper money for awhile longer. Actually,
what they proposed was a "trade."

The "deal" was as follows: For four days, citizens could
exchange their "old" dollars for the "new" currency, which
the consortium called "new credits." For three days, this
would be on a one-for-one basis: one old dollar got you one
new credit. On the fourth day, it would take *two* dollars to
receive one new credit. After the fourth day, the old dollars
were no longer legal tender. No financial institution would
accept them. No one could legally use them as payment for
goods or services. They were worthless pieces of paper.

The consortium also demanded that Congress pass legislation outlawing the private ownership of gold and silver.
In a concession to public opinion, they would allow Americans to convert their privately held gold and silver into new
credits…but only for four days.

In time, the consortium would phase out these new
credits in favor of the cashless debit card system, for the
debit card was their goal and their dream.

The consortium was positive that Congress would outlaw the use of the old dollars and the private ownership of
gold and silver. Therefore, the only remaining task was to
decide what punishment awaited those who chose to ignore
these laws.

The individuals behind the consortium were intelli-
gent—*and* they were patient. They knew that in time they

might need stiff penalties to back up these new statutes. For the present, though, they chose a "softer" approach: transgressors would be cited, then fined, but not jailed. The reason for this leniency was simple: The consortium knew that given enough time, and with perhaps a little gentle prodding, most Americans would accept their plan. They also knew that Americans did not like to be threatened, and that to threaten them with harsh punishment would simply cause unnecessary resistance to the new currency system by many otherwise compliant citizens. Also, by instituting severe penalties the consortium knew they ran the risk of open rebellion—perhaps even armed rebellion—by a sizable minority of the population. For these reasons, they instituted the less severe punishments.

Could the nation afford to say no to this "offer"? Most in Congress thought not. Only one Senator, from Wisconsin, and one Congresswoman, from California, sounded any alarm. Congress ignored these warnings—the nation's elected representatives were in no mood to debate this issue a second time. With overwhelming unanimity, both Houses passed the necessary legislation in less than thirty-six hours. President Storr signed the Bill into law the next day.

Ten days after the Market crash, the United States woke up to a new era: The "cashless" society was about to become reality.

Chapter Twenty
Broken Promises,
Shattered Dreams

From *Endtimes*: "The Dark Forces were clever and they were patient. Slowly, over the years and over the centuries, they spun their invisible web of control over the banks, over the governments, and over the major world corporations. By the nineteen nineties, they controlled these organizations as surely as if they owned them outright.

These entities had a vision—a grand and a dark vision—and the vision concerned the buying and the selling of human souls."

With the signing of the Debit Card Bill into law, the federal government admitted publicly what had been the truth for many years: The true locus of power did not reside in Washington; rather, it rested in the hands of little known individuals, individuals who owed allegiance to no country, no ethnic group, no religion—*individuals who owed allegiance to themselves and no one else.*

Shortly after the signing, the President and the Chairman of the Federal Reserve, in a joint press conference, announced a change in the government's economic policy. President Storr "admitted" that the government had "botched" the job of running the nation's economy. Only the private sector, he asserted, had the knowledge and the resources to bring the country out of the depression. The federal government did not. Therefore, he announced that the consortium of international bankers, the Federal Reserve, and the nation's major banks now had control — complete control — over the monetary and economic policy of the United States.

This change in policy completed the transfer of power — other groups now totally controlled the destiny of the country.

These groups decided they needed to create an image — a *positive* image — so they named themselves the "World Abundance Corporation." In time, they shortened this to the "Corporation." Everyone knew what it meant.

Did Americans realize the far-reaching implications of these changes? Those who did kept their understandings to themselves.

Meanwhile, the currency exchange proceeded as planned, and the public's response pleased the Corporation. According to their calculations, citizens had exchanged billions of "old" dollars and tons of gold and silver for new credits.

There was a hitch, however. In a top secret memo, circulated to no more than twenty individuals around the globe, the Corporation admitted that most of the gold and silver had not been redeemed for new credits. It remained in private hands. The Corporation did not comment extensively on this. They simply reminded Americans that Congress had outlawed the ownership of these precious metals.

Within the Corporation ranks, the membership disagreed about what to do about these privately held reserves. Some Corporation members, predicting that Americans would use these precious metals as money, and thus as a way to avoid joining the new currency system, wanted to institute immediate and severe penalties for the ownership of gold and silver. Others, more cautious, urged restraint. With an equal number on both sides, they decided to wait and to carefully monitor the situation.

Acting on Glenn's advice, Susan and Jeff had purchased a few thousand dollars worth of gold and silver, most of it in coins. When Congress outlawed the owning of these precious metals, Glenn had scoffed at the new law. "Gold and silver will be the only real money. You'll see," he'd stated.

They believed him...and they held onto their coins.

The new credits themselves were crisp and new and quite official-looking. The day after the Debit Card Law passed, banks around the country had a plentiful supply of the new bills. Clearly, someone had planned ahead—*way* ahead. Apparently, these same individuals had been very confident that Congress would enact the Debit Card Law.

Susan and Jeff turned in the little cash they had, more from curiosity than from any desire to own any of the new currency.

Jeff examined one of the new credits, turning it over in his hand. "What are these good for?" he asked the teller at the local bank where they had their account.

Shrugging her shoulders, the teller answered, "I guess you can use them like you would dollars. Most stores are taking them. I bought gas with mine this morning. But see, on the back it says they're only good for two weeks."

"What does *that* mean?" Susan asked.

"The new debit cards will be issued by then. Everyone's getting one you know. You'll get a number and a card. Then you'll have to turn your credits in so we can deposit them in your account. After that, you'll have to transact all your business with the debit card."

Jeff grimaced. "I'm not sure I like the sound of that. What do *you* think of this new system?" he asked the teller.

"It's the *law*," she replied curtly. "We don't have a choice."

Before they left the bank, Susan and Jeff witnessed a scene that was repeated thousands of times across the country in the next few days. It was a scene acted out by those who felt cheated and robbed and abandoned by the institutions they had trusted all their life.

Why were so many people upset? The reason was pretty simple: Most people who exchanged their dollars for new credits felt they had at least received *something* for their hard-earned money. But what about the billions of dollars that Americans had invested in CD's, in stocks, and in other "paper" wealth? The fate of this "money" was much less clear. Although the Corporation made vague promises to investigate the situation, they did little to follow through. It soon became obvious that those unlucky enough to have invested in this paper wealth had probably lost it.

Understandably, this upset many, many people.

Such was the case with the middle-aged couple who walked up to the window next to Susan and Jeff.

"Look," the man said, "I don't want any of these new whatever you call them. My wife and I have a twenty-five thousand dollar CD in your bank. *That's* what I want."

The teller sighed. She had heard the same or a similar story many times that morning. She felt emotionally and physically exhausted. "Mr. Williams, it's like I explained to you on the phone, we can't do anything *about* your CD. I wish we could, but we can't. It's gone. It happened when the bank failed. We're being told that there's no insurance to cover it. Lot's of folks lost their CD's you know. I'm truly sorry about yours," she said sympathetically.

The man's face reddened and he banged his fist on the counter. "What do you *mean* you can't do anything? What kind of dumbass answer is that?" he yelled. "We put that money in your bank. We *trusted* you. Now you say it's *gone?*"

The teller nodded. "I'm afraid so. It's really out of our control."

"Piss on that! It's our life savings! It's what we're going to buy our motor home with! Now you say we can't have it! Piss on that! And piss on you!"

The man's wife put her hand on his shoulder. "Now, Ted, she's doing the best she can. Aren't you, Miss? Perhaps we'll get it back later. Isn't that right, Miss? Won't the government look into this? They won't let everyone lose their money, will they? They'll do *something*, won't they?"

The teller shrugged her shoulders.

"The hell they will," the man muttered. "It's gone. I worked damn hard for that money...damn hard...all my life. Now it's gone. His shoulders sagged. "It was for our retirement." Tears rolled down his face. "It's gone." Without another word, he walked slowly away, leaving two of the new credits at the window.

Susan picked them up and handed them to the man. She put her arm around his shoulders in a silent gesture of support. The man didn't look up. He accepted the credits and left the bank.

Not everyone left as quietly as this man. People were angry and frustrated to learn that they had lost their life savings. Fair or not, the banks became the target of much of this anger.

People took their frustrations out on the tellers—verbally abusing them, threatening them, even physically assaulting them.

After awhile, the banks *themselves* became the target for the pent-up anger. Many a bank bore the scar of at least one broken window. Some were even bombed. And the incidence of bank holdups increased dramatically in the next few days.

The Chairman of the Federal Reserve, acting as a spokesman for the Corporation, appealed to the American people for calm and restraint. In eloquent and ringing tones, he asked that the Corporation be given a chance to bring order and stability and prosperity to the country. This, he stated, would take time. He decried the violence, warning it would only impede the Corporation's avowed goal of pulling the country out of the depression.

But Americans weren't listening to pleas for calm and restraint. The bank violence escalated.

The Corporation reacted swiftly.

Overnight, black-uniformed bank guards appeared across the country, one or two to every bank, savings and loan, and credit union. Mount Shasta had five of these guards. Dressed in black, with a police-type riot helmet and opaque black visor, each wore a large circular arm patch with the distinctive purple and white logo of the Corporation emblazoned in the center.

The Corporation called these guards "Prosperity Corps." They armed them with riot guns and instructed them to use them if they felt it was necessary.

Apparently the Prosperity Corps *did* consider it necessary to use their guns—on the first day they were stationed in the banks they killed one hundred and twenty-eight people. After that, the incidence of bank violence decreased sharply, and only those of a suicidal nature dared to vent their anger against these financial institutions.

Did the killing of civilians upset Washington? If so, it was not obvious. The White House called for restraint by the guards, but federal prosecutors announced that they had no plans to press charges against any member of the Prosperity Corps who killed someone "in the line of duty." The following day, the Secretary of the Interior stated that although he understood the anger and the frustration felt by those who had lost their savings, this was no excuse for harassing bank employees or for destroying private property.

It appeared to many Americans that a foreign power had invaded the United States, a foreign power whose identity was yet unknown.

Chapter Twenty-One
Life at the Sunshine Cafe

Revelations: 21:3 And I heard a great voice out of heaven saying, Behold, the tabernacle of God is with men, and he will dwell with them, and they shall be his people, and God himself shall be with them and be their God.

═══════════════════════════

When Susan and Jeff arrived at the Sunshine Cafe two days later, this newly made sign in the front window greeted them:

Hello friends and patrons!
Yes, we are open!
But the old money is no good now. (Was it ever?) So here is how we are doing business. We will *not* accept the new credits until/unless we absolutely *have* to. Same for the debit card when it comes (beware of the Mark of the Beast, friends). We *will* accept gold or silver. What? You don't have any gold or silver? Okay, then we'll accept trades—fresh vegetables especially welcome. If you don't have anything to trade, come on in anyway and we'll work something out.
Love and Light and Peace,
The Management

After reading the sign, Susan turned to Jeff. "Bring any fresh veggies in that spiffy new coat?" she teased, referring to the mallard blue jacket Jeff was proudly wearing.

"Nope. I knew I forgot something."

"Want to wash dishes to work off your morning bagel? I'll dry."

"Nope. You know how my hands hate detergent."

"Well...?"

"I brought six of our silver quarters. We can get all the bagels we want and have enough left over to take one home to Sam."

"He hates onion remember."

"Right," Jeff said. Reaching into his pocket for the quarters, he silently thanked Glenn. At first he'd thought Glenn was smart, advising them to put their cash into gold and silver coins. Then, when the government outlawed the owning of these coins, he'd regretted buying them. Now it seemed that maybe Glenn had been right; maybe gold and silver would always be worth something...no matter what the government did. At least they could eat at the Sunshine Cafe—probably for life.

"Hey, man."

Jeff turned around to see a tall thin man with penetrating black eyes staring at him.

"You got some silver quarters, huh? Lucky you," the man said. Dressed in a tattered olive overcoat, with unwashed, matted hair, he looked like one of the Mount Shasta "street people" who often frequented the tiny cafe.

Jeff tensed, "Well...we have a few," he answered cautiously, feeling a sudden stab of fear. Maybe the man was harmless...maybe...but his dull, hard eyes bored right into Jeff and he was anxious. "A few. Just a few," he repeated.

Susan had been watching this scene. "You need some money? Jeff, give him one of our quarters. We have enough."

Jeff hesitated. "Ah...I don't know..."

"I do. Here," Susan said, handing the man one of the silver quarters. "Enjoy."

A smile instantly softened the man's face. "Thanks. I wasn't asking you know. It's just I woke up today and found out my money is pretty worthless. Not that I had lots to begin with, course." His smile widened, revealing teeth that badly needed work.

"Why didn't you turn your money in?" Jeff asked.

"Been up on the Mountain on a vision quest. First I heard about this money thing was this morning when I came down for supplies. Bank told me it was too late to get my money changed. Told me I should've done it sooner. Got a dog I have to feed, too. Don't rightly know what I'm going to do about her," he said, frowning.

Handing the man another quarter, Jeff said, "Here, take this, we can't let your dog go hungry."

"Thanks again. Much obliged. What goes around comes around. You'll be repaid, Brother."

"Sure." Now that his initial wave of fear had passed, Jeff rather liked the man. He guessed that the hardness he'd first seen in the man's eyes was fear. It must be very upsetting to discover that the money you thought would buy food was now worthless. At least he and Susan had their gold and silver. Enough for awhile anyway...quite awhile if they were careful. Many people, like this man, had nothing. "You want to join us for breakfast?" Jeff asked. Then, remembering Susan, he said, "That okay with you, sweetie?"

"Great. I'd like to hear about your vision quest," she said to the man.

They opened an account with the four remaining quarters. The young woman behind the counter handed Jeff a credit slip for twelve dollars and fifty cents, based on the value of the silver in the coins. He and Susan ordered bagels and two cups of the strong, dark coffee the cafe was famous for. Their newly acquired friend had a freshly baked blueberry muffin and tea. Jeff insisted on paying for the man's breakfast. Handing the credit slip to the young woman, she subtracted four dollars and eighty cents and returned it to him.

They sat down at a window table. "What's your name?" Susan asked the man.

"Andrew," he replied, removing his coat and folding it neatly on the chair beside him.

Taking a bite of her bagel, she asked, "And where are you from, Andrew?"

"Oh, here and there," Andrew answered vaguely. "Me and my dog, we travel around the country doing the Lord's work."

Although he was now much more comfortable with Andrew, Jeff hoped they weren't going to get a sermon or a speech about the end of the world. For some reason, Andrew had that feel to him.

Susan leaned forward and asked, "And what *is* the Lord's work, Andrew?"

Jeff nudged her foot under the table, hoping she would take it as a signal not to ask Andrew any more questions along that line. Andrew grinned at Jeff as if he knew *exactly* what he had been thinking.

Andrew very carefully began cutting up his muffin. "The Lord's work? Oh, talking to nice people like you. Networking the God energy. Telling folks what's happening in different parts of the country."

Andrew talked so slowly and so deliberately, Jeff wondered if he might be slightly retarded. Who did Andrew remind him of? He was trying to remember when a commotion at the next table interrupted his thoughts.

A man in a red and black checkered lumber jacket pounded on the table. "Shit! You think this shit-assed government cares about us?" he asked angrily. He didn't wait for a reply from his friends. "I say we got to take care of ourselves! What's going to happen when those city folks run outta money and food? How long before they figure it out that we got land and food and good clean water up here?" he asked, glaring at the others. "Huh? How long before they start heading up the Interstate and take what we got? You think this shit-assed government's going to stop them? Shit no! I say we gotta take care of ourselves!" Glancing furtively around, he lowered his voice, but his angry words still boomed out across the small cafe. "It's simple. We get us some dynamite and set some charges on those fancy new I-5 bridges. If the time comes, we blow the hell out of the freeway. That'll slow them down," he chuckled.

"But a lot will still get through," someone argued.

"Then we take care of them," the man growled menacingly. "Knock a few of the bastards off. The rest will get the message. You bet."

Reading the man's energy, Susan detected much fear. The anger was a cover-up. How many others had his fear?

Susan turned to Andrew and asked, "Andrew, what do *you* think about all that's happened in the past few days? The new money...and those kinds of things?"

"Oh, it's all shaking out," Andrew replied cryptically.

Susan raised her eyebrows. "Shaking out?"

"It's happening like it's supposed to. The good Lord didn't put us in charge of what's going on, so why bust our brains trying to understand it?" He grinned. "I seen a lot in the past few years, traveling around the country. I don't try to understand it no more. I just talk to people and get them to think love thoughts. If enough of them do that, I figure everything's going to be okay. I guess that might sound kind of stupid to some folks, but I seen it work lots of times. Anyhow, it's what the good Lord's told me to do, so I do it. It makes me happy."

"I don't think it's stupid at all, Andrew," Susan replied. "I think it's wonderful what you do."

"Thanks," Andrew mumbled, lowering his eyes as if Susan's words embarrassed him. "I don't take no credit for it. I do it because it's the Lord's work."

Susan had one more question. "What if you meet people who are angry at life?"

"You mean like them?" Andrew replied, glancing at the group at the adjacent table. "I'd let them talk. Some folks just need to get pissed for awhile. Sometimes they get over it. Course, if I can get a word in edgewise, I tell them how lucky they are to be alive and to be here on this beautiful Mother Earth."

Jeff looked puzzled. "Why are they so lucky?"

"You don't know?"

"I guess not."

"Because the Lord is coming back to Earth. He's com-ing soon."

"That would be great," was all Jeff could think of to say.

"You don't believe me, do you?"

"Uh...I'm not sure."

The look that Andrew gave him sent chills up and down Jeff's spine. It was the same look Susan gave him every now and then—the look of pure *knowing*.

"You're a nice man, but you don't really *believe*. Your wife does, though. It doesn't matter. People don't have to believe. It's going to happen anyway. The Lord's coming anyway." He got up to leave. "I thank you for the money. Be seeing you around."

"Maybe some time you can tell us about your vision quest and some more about the work you do," Susan sug-gested.

"Sure," Andrew said as he walked away.

Watching him go, Jeff knew Andrew was right—he *didn't* believe...not the way he *wanted* to.

Chapter Twenty-Two
Power Centers

From *Endtimes*: "We have talked before about the idea of power centers. To re-fresh your memory, power centers are those places on the Planet that possess extraordinarily high concentrations of healing energy.

Now, let us speak again of those Dark Forces who dreamed of owning the Earth. Among these entities, the concept of power centers was a hotly debated is-sue. Some maintained that this idea was only in the minds of a few, far out, fringe-type spiritual seekers, and of no concern, and certainly no danger, to their plans for world domination.

Others, not convinced, delved into the ancient records, records that were not available to the average citizen of Planet Earth, and they discovered that there was indeed *something* different about these places."

Three days after Jeff and Susan's meeting with Andrew and seven days after Congress passed the Debit Card Law, the Corporation announced that they had begun shipping the debit cards to the regional distribution centers. In California, the distribution center was the Bank of the Western United States.

Although obviously well organized, nevertheless, for the Corporation to create, print, and distribute millions of these debit cards in seven short days was quite an amazing feat. An *impossible* feat some thought.

How could the Corporation have pulled off this organizational miracle?

They didn't. Most Americans had had a debit card waiting for them for several *years*.

The Corporation announced that everyone had a week to pick up their card and to deposit any new credits into their account.

The Corporation also announced that by the end of the month all banks and other financial institutions would close down. Except for the bank issuing the card—this bank would remain open to help resolve any possible disputes and to act as the Corporation's agent.

Finally, the Corporation reminded citizens that the only *legal* way to do business in the United States was by using the debit card, and that the use of any other means—credit cards, checking accounts, gold or silver, or bartering and trading of any kind—would result in citations and possible fines.

These announcements came through the Corporation. Except for a brief statement urging each citizen to do his or her part in these difficult times, to accept the new card, and to be patient as the Corporation ironed out the glitches in the new system, Washington was silent.

The worry about "glitches" proved needless, however. Those who picked up their cards found that businesses accepted the new debit card just as willingly as they had the older credit cards. In some ways, transactions with the new card were even easier. Most of the larger stores already had the newly installed debit card computer terminals. Buying something was now as "simple" as inserting the card into the terminal and having the computer automatically subtract the amount of the purchase from the customer's debit card account.

President Storr had been correct: There were no checks to write, no long, frustrating bank lines to wait in, and no paperwork.

The system worked so well that the Corporation decided to hook *all* stores, even the smallest, into the new system.

The debit card handled more than just the buying and selling of merchandise, however. It also processed all money that was earned in the workplace. Employers now fed their employee wages into the computer system. The computer automatically deducted all appropriate taxes, along with such diverse items as unpaid traffic tickets and child support payments, then credited the remainder to the employee's debit card account.

The same system governed those in business for themselves. Since hiring a plumber, visiting a dentist, or having your car repaired at the local garage now had to be paid for with the debit card, self-employed earnings could be treated the same as wages.

Much thought and much planning had gone into this new system, and the planning paid off. By midweek, reports emanating from the Corporation's Virginia headquarters were positively glowing. In fewer than three days, more than half the eligible people had picked up their cards, and exit polls at selected banks showed that an overwhelming percentage of these people approved of the new system.

Although most of the country welcomed the card, a few places did not. Mount Shasta was one such place.

"I don't want one," Susan said, referring to the debit card.

Jeff shrugged his shoulders. "Okay, no problem. Only it might come in handy every now and then. It's not like we'd *have* to use it if we didn't want to."

Susan grinned. "You remember what we both said about our first bank credit card?"

Jeff shook his head no.

"We said we were only getting it for identification. Remember? We weren't actually going to *buy* anything with it. Oh no, not us. We weren't going to fall into *that* trap. It was pay with cash or do without. That was our motto. Remember?"

Jeff scratched his head and laughed. "Ah...now that you mention it I do recall a conversation along those lines."

"How long before our good intentions went right out the window?"

"Oh, a few months."

"*Two*."

"It was a great stereo, though."

"I agree, but remember what happened? We got *hooked* on that credit card. Sometimes we had the cash in our pockets and we *still* used it."

"There was something kind of addictive about that little piece of plastic, wasn't there?"

"So let's not take the card. Let's use our gold and silver instead."

"Sure...except it *is* illegal."

"That's true, but how many people do you know who have been cited for using gold or silver?"

"Only a couple," Jeff admitted. "But they could get really serious about this."

"They could...but it seems like they're afraid of something, so I think we're okay for now. But if you don't want to use our coins, we can trade for what we want. Lots of people are doing that." While shopping in Mount Shasta, Susan had seen a flyer for a new barter club. She thought it was a wonderful idea, and she was making a list of things she could use for trade. "And I'm going to start a garden. Yum. Fresh veggies. Doesn't that sound good? Evelyn's going to help. She's not taking the card, either. Neither is Anna. Lots of people aren't."

Jeff knew other people who weren't accepting the card,

although he imagined many of them would eventually change their minds. Not Susan, however.

"A garden does sound good. We might need a greenhouse, though. The growing season is pretty short up here."

"Great! I've always wanted to build a greenhouse. I bet we can get lots of people to help," Susan said enthusiastically. Then a serious look came over her face. "You know, I keep coming back to the thought that we don't *have* to take this card. We *really don't*. We don't have to be part of the debit card system, and we don't have to be a part of any of the other changes that are coming. None of it feels good to me, so I'm going to say "no thanks.""

"Me too."

Susan sighed. "Still, in a way I'm glad all this has happened. Does that sound weird?"

"Mm...no...except there's too many changes for me. I'd like things to go slower."

"Things moving too fast for you are they, sweetie?" Susan teased.

Jeff laughed. He held up his hand and counted on his fingers: "Let's see, the weather is doing really strange things, the President is killed, we've got a new President who looks like he's not really alive, an earthquake wipes out half of the state of California, the country is in the worst depression ever, and now the debit card. I mean, what's next?"

Susan had a mischievous twinkle in her eye. "If you really want to know..."

"No wait, sorry I asked."

"Okay, I'll spare you the gory details," Susan replied, a grin on her face. Then she was quiet for a moment. "It *is* pretty unsettling, though, isn't it? Sometimes I think about all the people who have died or who have lost everything they worked so hard for. I wonder...why does it have to be like this? Why so much suffering? The only thing that helps is to remember that it's everyone's choice and that it's part of their destiny path. Still..."

"Yeah. It's hard to understand."

"And sometimes I have doubts about how we're going to make it," Susan admitted.

"You *do*?" Jeff looked like he didn't quite believe her.

"Sure."

"Then why did you say you were glad this happened?"

"Because another part of me knows that this is a gift...even if it doesn't *look* like it. It's a gift because when everything comes apart like this, it shakes you up. And *that* can be a great motivator."

"I know you've told me this before, but honestly, sometimes this stuff goes through my brain like it was a sieve," Jeff said. "So tell me again what you mean."

"Sure. The way I see it these kinds of events come into our lives to wake us up. They challenge us to see our limitations—our *self-imposed* limitations. You know, those pictures we carry around that say we can't do this and we can't have that. Then, when we can recognize our self-imposed limitations, we have the option to change them. Know what I mean?"

"Ah, sort of."

"Okay, remember when you and I met? Remember how scared we were to be in a committed relationship?"

"Uh-huh. I went through lots of sleepless nights during that time."

"So did I. We were *scared* that if we committed ourselves to the relationship we'd lose our freedom."

Jeff made a face. "I felt like I was about to be sentenced to life imprisonment without the possibility of parole."

Susan laughed. "Me too. But guess what I discovered? I discovered that I didn't have to give up *anything* to be in this relationship. That was just a fear picture I carried around with me. The way things turned out, I didn't lose *any* freedom. In fact, I'm more free now than I was before, because the commitment I thought I was making to you and to us was actually to *me*; and when I made that commitment to me, I found a part of myself that had been missing for a long time. I wish I could explain it better than that, but I can't." Susan sighed. "Anyway, now I know there are *other* pieces of me missing. I want to find them. I want to know who I am. I want to *remember*. And I will. I *intend* to."

"I never thought of it like that. But you're right, I've found a freedom, too."

Susan continued, "What it took for us to find our freedom was the *challenge*. There we were in each other's lives. We knew we wanted to be together, but we also knew that we'd have to make some changes, and a part of us didn't want to. We wanted the relationship, but the changes seemed scary. It was a *challenge*. The challenge was to have the relationship *and* our freedom. We had to stop and think. We had to examine our lives, and then we had to change some of our pictures of reality. *We had to decide what kind of lives we wanted*." Susan stopped to gather her thoughts. Breathing deeply of the clean mountain air, she gazed out over the deck, at the trees and the flowers, and then up at her beloved Mountain, the Mountain that always filled her heart with such magic. "The Stock Market crash, the debit card, even the President being killed and the quake, it's a gift, and it's going to challenge us to think about our pictures of reality. Maybe some people won't be ready. Many will, though, and it will be good, because we'll find pieces of ourselves that have been missing for a long, long time. And then we can create the kind of life that's an expression of our highest possibility."

Jeff didn't see Susan's vision as clearly as she did, but listening to her these past few weeks, he was beginning to believe that if they had the courage to follow their path and to step into the unknown, they would be guided and they would be protected.

Chapter Twenty-Three
Mount Shasta Says No !

From *Endtimes*: "What was so special about these power centers?

When the Dark Forces studied these spiritual locations, they found, among other things, statistically significant differences in the electromagnetic fields surrounding these areas.

And the inhabitants? Many were immune to the kind of mind control techniques that worked so well on other portions of the general population. This greatly worried the Dark Forces, for if even a *few* human beings were immune to their mind control technology then their dream of world domination might be in great danger.

Mount Shasta was one such power center."

The individuals running the Corporation knew with extraordinary precision who was accepting the card and who wasn't, and they did not like what they saw. Specifically, it was the *pattern* of acceptance that worried them. It worried them enough that they sent out a call to the farthest corners of the globe, summoning the brethren to meet at their Virginia retreat to plan their strategy.

What did the numbers show? They showed that while the overwhelming majority of city dwellers were accepting the card, many in the rural areas were not. The numbers were 85 percent acceptance in the cities and only 55 percent in the countryside.

Why such a big difference? Glenn had been right— many in the cities viewed the debit card as simply another credit card and did not question it. Some *did* question it but still accepted it. These individuals felt they had little choice: They had to feed their families, pay their bills, and put gas in the car. From their point of view, it was either accept the card or do without some basic necessities.

And in truth, some characteristics of city life did make refusal of the card difficult. For instance, although many city dwellers had stockpiled gold and silver, and although the penalties for using it remained minimal, spending it to buy things proved almost impossible. The supermarkets and the chain stores, acting on orders from corporate head-quarters, refused to accept these precious metals as payment for goods and services. So did most fast food establishments and most gas stations.

Another aspect of city life that made refusal of the card difficult was the almost total dependence on some form of cash—urban dwellers *bought* what they needed. They did not grow their own food, nor did they barter or trade. They operated in a cash economy, and the debit card was now the only "cash" in town.

Not so in the countryside. Here, people felt they had choices.

Individuals in these areas were more receptive to the idea of using gold and silver as currency. Perhaps it was a holdover from pioneer days; or perhaps it was simply that many rural dwellers had always mistrusted "paper" money and now jumped at the chance to use "real" money again. Whatever the reason, those who had purchased gold and silver found it readily accepted by many local businesses.

Also, most rural areas already had a flourishing barter

and trade network. In the next few days, these networks grew enormously as more and more people turned to them to obtain the necessities of life.

And it was a rare country home that did not have a small garden, or at least space for one.

For these reasons, rural America felt more secure in refusing the card.

Of course, many in the countryside accepted the card without hesitation, as many in the city had done. But many did not, and by the second week, it was apparent to the Corporation that they had a problem.

The individuals running the Corporation were extraordinary planners, and they expected their plans to work. Frustrated by the spotty success of the card, they acted swiftly to remedy the situation. The meeting at their Virginia retreat was brief. They quickly agreed to a plan of action. There was very little debate.

Their next press release was also brief. The new monetary policy, it stated, would not work unless the debit card achieved a 99 percent acceptance rate. Although expressing pleasure at the 85 percent rate in the cities, it severely criticized rural America for its halfhearted acceptance. The average rate for the countryside, it tersely pointed out, was still only 55 percent; for Northern California, 45 percent; for the small Northern California mountain town of Mount Shasta, 35 percent. Mount Shasta took the prize for having the lowest rate in the country. Sedona, Arizona, was close with a 36 percent.

The figures for rural America, the Corporation warned, were not good enough—these "non complying" regions must rethink their ways.

Initially, the only pressure applied to the wayward rural areas was a subtle media campaign. Reporters wrote stories portraying their residents as well meaning, but ill advised. The underlying assumption was that as soon as the "refusniks" saw the "bigger picture"—as soon as they considered what was *best for the country*—they would fall into line and take the card. Groups of school children from across the United States wrote letters to the local papers in these areas, asking people to be good citizens and good Americans and accept the card. An aging and obviously ill Billy Graham devoted a prime time television special to the same theme.

Many people saw the Corporation's hand in this media campaign.

This gentle approach met with only limited success. Rural America raised its rate to 59 percent; Northern California to 48 percent. In Mount Shasta, the rate actually *fell* to 33 percent. Apparently, Mount Shastans resented the pressure to conform...even if the pressure was subtle.

The Corporation decided that sterner measures were necessary. They announced that non complying areas had three days to raise their acceptance rate to 85 percent. After that, all state and federal funds would be cut off.

Those in the countryside either did not believe these threats or they did not care, because the acceptance rates did not budge.

The Corporation waited three days. Then, acting under special provisions granted them by Congress as a part of the Debit Card Law, they ordered state and federal agencies to stop the flow of funds to the non complying areas.

This action struck a nerve with local officials. The Corporation obviously meant what it said. These rural bureaucrats saw a bleak future for themselves and their districts. In fact, with no government funding of *any* kind, they saw themselves *out of business*.

They panicked.

In Mount Shasta, where the compliance rate was still the lowest in the country, the *Mount Shasta Tribune* devoted its next edition to a fiery discussion of the debit card situation. Impassioned pleas by the mayor, the city council, county officials, and local citizens urged their neighbors to accept the card. A special full-page editorial predicted economic disaster if the citizens of the town continued their stubborn ways.

The Corporation fired one more shot. They announced that they were seriously considering the physical takeover of the worst offending areas. *This meant the actual replacement of city and county personnel by federal officials.* Local autonomy would cease to exist.

The morning edition of the *San Francisco Ledger* published a list of areas that were prime takeover targets.

The city of Mount Shasta headed the list.

Jeff finished reading the *Ledger* story. He handed the paper to Susan.

"Hm," she said, putting down the paper, "things are moving fast."

"You think they'll really do this? Come in and take over?"

"Yes, they'll do it. They don't make idle threats."

"I can't believe they'd actually send the Feds in."

"The Corporation," Susan said, saying the word slowly, reading its energy. "I wonder who they are?"

Jeff picked up the paper. "There's a list here someplace. Let's see there's the Federal Reserve and..."

Susan interrupted him. "No, I mean who are they *really?*"

"Oh," Jeff said, not quite understanding.

"They are so *smart*. Smart and methodical and patient. They have thought this through so carefully. You can almost *feel* the thought they've put into their plans. Yes, they'll do it. They have decided they need an example to show the rest of the country, and we're *it.*"

Chapter Twenty-Four
The Gathering

Revelations: 16:19: And the great city was divided into three parts, and the cities of the nation fell: And great Babylon came in remembrance before God, to give unto her the cup of the wine of the fierceness of his wrath.

After only a brief stay in Mount Shasta, Susan and Jeff had quickly discovered that their new neighbors loved to speak out on issues that concerned them. They learned that it was common for local residents to pack City Hall during the discussion of some important piece of town business; and that it was also common for the city council to move the meeting to larger quarters when it was clear that there were more interested people than the old, cramped facilities could accommodate.

So they were not surprised when two days later, as they were having lunch at the Sunshine Cafe, a man stood up and reported that the City Council had scheduled a special town meeting to discuss the government's rumored takeover of Mount Shasta.

"Seven PM, at the high school," the man announced. The cafe regulars loudly cheered him as he sat down.

"We'll be there!" shouted several of the cafe's patrons.

Susan and Jeff also decided to attend.

Word of such events travels quickly in a small town; by 6:30, Mount Shastans had packed the high school gym. Jeff estimated that at least 500 people had crammed themselves into the old, worn bleachers, with another one hundred or so standing or sitting on the floor.

Jeff and Susan squeezed in between a young woman in a red dress, who Susan thought worked at the town's library, and an elderly, white haired man with a clip board perched on his lap. Glancing around, Susan spied Evelyn and Veda sitting three rows away. She also spotted the man in the red and black checkered jacket who had so angrily denounced the government in the Sunshine Cafe a few days before. Scanning the rest of the audience, she saw many "average" citizens. Reading their energies, she sensed tenseness and fear in many of them.

On the floor of the gym, seated around a long oval table, three men and two women nervously shuffled papers and occasionally leaned over to talk to each other. Susan didn't recognize them. Neither did Jeff.

One of the men, a balding man of fifty or so, moved the microphone in front of him, then tapped it to make sure it was working. "Okay folks, I guess we can get started. For those of you who don't know, I'm Stan Morrisey. I'm your mayor, and these folks seated here with me are your elected city council."

A smattering of boos met Morrisey's introduction. Someone threw a wadded-up piece of paper onto the floor of the gym. It rolled next to Mayor Morrisey's foot. He picked up the paper and placed it on the table. The booing continued. He raised his hands to quiet the crowd. "Okay, okay. Let's save the political comments for later."

The air in the gym crackled with tension. Susan felt this tension begin to build up in her body. It made her uncomfortable; she shifted around in her seat to move the energy.

"Who the hell appointed *you* leader of this meeting!" someone yelled at the mayor.

"Nobody I guess...but somebody's got to do it. *You* want the job?" the mayor spat back at the heckler.

"I'll sure as hell think about it!" the man yelled. "If you don't do a better job running this meeting than you do running the damn town, you bet I will!" he added angrily.

Glancing apprehensively around the packed gym, the mayor said, "I realize we're all a little on edge. You should see what it's like at City Hall these days." He laughed. "That's a joke, in case you didn't get it." No one laughed. He cleared his throat. "Seriously now, let's see if we can conduct this meeting in a polite and half civilized manner. Okay? Most of you know what's going on. We've had to convert to a new currency system, and…"

"Bullshit! Who said we *had* to?"

The voice had come from in back of Susan. She turned around, half expecting to see the angry man from the cafe, but it was a rather average looking fellow in horn-rimmed glasses.

The mayor's face visibly reddened. "Well…I guess that's a matter of opinion. But what's done is done. We have this new debit card now, and that's the way it is. Only I guess a lot of you don't want to go along with it."

"Damn right we don't!" This time it *was* the man from the cafe.

"Right," the mayor responded, taking a deep breath, obviously trying to control himself. "Ah…we received this directive today," he said, holding up a piece of paper, his hand shaking badly. "This comes from the Corporation, and it has the Seal of the United States of America on it." The mention of the United States elicited a few scattered boos. Waiting until the noise subsided, the mayor continued, "It says we have *got* to comply with the new law. This means a lot of you are going to have to switch to the debit card. Otherwise, the Feds are coming in and taking over," he added, waving the paper in front of him. "They mean it folks! They've already cut off all city and county funds! Do you want the Feds in here taking control of our city?" he asked angrily.

"No! No Feds!" many in the crowd yelled back.

"So what if they send in the damn Feds? They can't make us take their card! We don't *have* to take it! They can't *make* us!" the man from the cafe shouted. Lusty cheers and an equal number of boos greeted his remarks.

"Yes they *can!*" the mayor yelled back. He banged his fist on the table, tipping over the water glass beside the microphone. "Somebody get me a rag, would you?" he asked half under his breath. Wiping up the water, he said, "I'm afraid you're *wrong*, sir—they *can* make us. How long do you think we can survive without any state or federal funds? I checked with our county administrator. He says two months. *Maybe*. Look, that money pays for the Highway Patrol, and right now we don't have any of those guys out there on the freeway *protecting* us."

Almost everyone loudly cheered this announcement. Even the mayor smiled. "Oh, I get it. I don't like them either sometimes. But that money also pays for the county sheriffs. What will we do when there are no more sheriff's patrols? And the road work, *that* won't get done either. I bet you won't like it when you run your truck into a big pothole on Mount Shasta Boulevard. Come on, folks, let's be practical. We *need* that money!"

"Mr. Mayor!" A tall, frail looking man got up painfully slowly, supporting himself with a cane. "My name's Ned Fortus. I run the sporting goods store in town. One of them anyway."

Mayor Morrisey smiled. "Sure, Ned. Everybody knows you. Everybody who's ever bought a fishing pole anyway. How are you?" The mayor seemed relieved to be talking to a "friend."

"Fine, Mr. Mayor, except for this here leg," Ned replied. "I want to say something, and I know there are lots of folks who agree with me. We think you're doing a great job...and well...that's about all I have to say about that."

Ned's endorsement instantly brought more boos and cheers. The mayor held up his hand. "This isn't a popularity contest. We have serious business here tonight. Anything else you want to say, Ned?"

Ned shifted to his other leg. "It's just I can't stay in business unless people start using this new debit card. I got to pay my taxes and I got to pay my suppliers...and its gotta be done with this new card. It's the only way. I can't do it any other way. It's easy to use the card. They installed one of those new processors in my store. It's easy. You just slip your card in and that's all there is to it. Anyhow, if you care about the businesses in your town, well, you'll take this card. I got mine. There's nothing to it."

"Thanks, Ned, we appreciate your comments. Anyone else?" the Mayor asked.

A portly middle aged man stood up. "Yeah, I guess I'll say something. Name's Walt and I live on the south end of town off Old Stage. I haven't taken the card, and I *won't*!" Walt grinned and held up his arms in a victory salute, acknowledging the cheers from the audience. "Only thing is, I'm having a little trouble buying my beans and bacon. Me and my wife went down to the market, and the clerk told me I had to have this card if I wanted to buy anything from his store. I told him I didn't have one, but that I would make him a trade. Told him I'd trade my wife here for a year's worth of groceries. But he didn't go for it. Anyone here want to take me up on this?" He grinned. The woman siting next to him tugged frantically on his coat to get him to sit down.

There were a few chuckles here and there. Mostly, though, people ignored Walt's attempted levity. They shifted around in their seats. They stretched. They glanced around at each other. They seemed eager to get down to the real issues that had brought them together this evening.

Chapter Twenty-Five
Susan Speaks Out

Revelations: 21:1: And I saw a new heaven and a new earth: for the first heaven and the first earth were passed away; and there was no more sea.

"Can I say something?"

Susan turned around and looked up to see a young woman, dressed in jeans and a tee shirt, holding up her hand.

"Sure," the mayor replied amiably.

"My name is Nancy. I don't actually live in your town. I'm here visiting friends." She paused, nervously clearing her throat. "I'm a photographer, and I want to tell you what's happening in Los Angeles. Do you know what's happening down there?"

The Mayor held up his hand to stop her. "Now wait a minute, that's a little off the subject," he protested.

"Come on, let her speak!" someone yelled.

Nancy reached down and picked something up from the floor in front of her. "I've just come back from Los Angeles. I won't tell you how I got down there...I mean how I got through the barricades...because it's a secret I want to keep for now. Besides, someone helped me get through, and I don't want to get him in trouble.

"I was there for the last two weeks. I saw things and...I...have photos...if you want to see them." She stopped to wipe away the tears streaming down her face. "Everyone is lying to you. They say everything is getting back to normal and that people are being taken care of. It's a lie." She stopped again to blow her nose. "I just wanted to let you know what's going on," she said, and started to sit back down.

"Wait! Tell us more!" the woman sitting next to her pleaded. "I have a friend down there."

"I have a sister there!"

"My mom and dad live there!"

Nancy stood back up. "Most of the cities have been bulldozed. They're just not there anymore. But they aren't *telling* you this. And the pictures you see on TV—the ones showing people rebuilding their homes? It's not true. It's a lie. The cities aren't there anymore. The *houses* aren't there anymore. *Nothing's* there. Something else they haven't told you about are the mass graves. The army dug huge pits and stacked people in and threw gas on them and burned them and shoveled dirt on them.

"Another thing you don't know about are the concentration camps. The troops rounded up all the survivors and herded them into camps. They won't let them leave. They shoot anyone who tries to escape."

"Why?" several people wanted to know.

Nancy shrugged her shoulders. "Maybe they saw something they weren't supposed to see. Maybe the army doesn't want them to talk about it."

Someone else asked, "We heard rumors about the nuclear plant at San Luis Obispo. Did it really explode?"

"I'm not sure. I heard that it's leaking pretty bad, but...Ah...that's all I know." Nancy replied as she sat back down.

Susan leaned close to Jeff. "I believe her."

Jeff nodded his head. "So do I."

Except for a few scattered coughs, the room was quiet.

"Anyone else want to speak?" a tired looking Mayor Morrisey asked.

Susan stood up. "I want to say that I'm not taking the card. In my opinion, it's a trick, and it's not my intention to be tricked anymore. I also want to say that if you're afraid you can't make it without this card, that's not the truth. You *can*. There's lots of ways. We can help each other. Maybe that's what this is about. Maybe Spirit is teaching us how to help each other." She stopped, not quite knowing what to say. She spied Evelyn and Veda smiling at her. Many others were, too. "I think it would be great if we got together and talked about what's happening. Let's *support* each other. It's easy to feel alone...and we're not.

"It's also easy to get confused. In fact, some people *want* us confused. These people have a plan. They have their own ideas about things. They aren't *my* ideas, and maybe they aren't yours either, but I guess that's another story. Anyway, these individuals..."

"The Gray Men!" someone shouted.

"What?"

"The Gray Men! That's who you're talking about!"

"Thanks. That's a good name for them. Okay, then, the *Gray Men* don't want anyone getting in the way of their plans. So they'd like us to believe that we're alone, because if we believe we're alone, then it's easy to scare us into believing that we can't refuse their card. But you see, the truth is, we're *not* alone. So let's get together and support each other. Let's get a sign-up sheet going around. We can meet at my house."

"I have a notebook. I'll start passing it around," the woman at the end of Susan's row volunteered.

Susan smiled in appreciation. "Great. Thanks."

The Mayor shifted around nervously in his chair. "I see lots of hands up, so who's next?"

A man on the other side of the gymnasium stood up and said to Susan, "I'd like to thank you for saying these things. They are my thoughts exactly. Thanks. I'd also like to sign up, and I'd like to help in any way I can. I would also..."

"You people are full of shit!" yelled an elderly man at the far end of the gym. "You are undermining this country! That woman who says she has pictures, she's..."

The Mayor pounded his gavel. "Wait a minute, wait a minute, you can't just interrupt someone like that! You'll have your chance to..."

"Bullshit! They're traitors! I fought in the war! I'm a vet. I have a right to speak—and by god I'm *going* to!"

The Mayor put down his gavel, giving up his attempt to quiet the man.

"That woman who says she has pictures, she's lying! What she says is happening, it's *not* happening that way! You're a god damned liar!" he yelled across the room at Nancy.

Nancy jumped to her feet. "No, I'm *not* lying! You want to see the pictures? Come and see them!" she yelled defiantly.

"You are, too, goddamn it. You're lying! You fixed those pictures! You're lying about my government and my country! They should lock you up for the things you're saying! I was in the army! I fought in World War Two! I know about the army! They wouldn't do those things! You're making it up!"

"Oh no I'm not! I saw what I saw! And I have proof right here!" Nancy yelled, waving the photographs in front of her.

"Bullshit! I don't believe it!" the man shouted. "And you," he yelled, pointing at Susan, "where do you get off saying we don't have to take this card? Who in the hell are *you* to question this? You think you're smarter than the government? You sound like one of those goddamned airy-fairy hippies we have running around here." Many in the audience booed and hissed his remarks. "Why don't you go the hell back where you came from and quit making trouble. This used to be a nice place to live...a *nice* place...until *you* people moved in. Get the hell out of this town!"

"Do you honestly think we're causing all the problems?" Susan asked.

"Damn right! I know who you are. I've seen you around town. You hang out with those other weirdo kooks. You're all into devil worship. That's why all this is happening—the earthquakes and the flooding. It's retribution for what you're doing. You're *evil*! All of you! You're *evil*!"

The waves of fear and anger coming from this man momentarily overwhelmed her, and she was too stunned to reply. Then, suddenly, she felt her fear being triggered. It was the old, familiar fear that others would hurt her for speaking her truth. It did not help to remind herself that times were different and that it was now safe to say what was in her heart, for her fear was not a logical fear that she could persuade to leave by an appeal to reason. It was deep within her emotional body—it was deep within her *soul memory*—and no logical argument would dissolve it.

Taking a deep breath, Susan said, "I'm sorry you feel that way. I only meant to help. Maybe if..."

"I don't need your help! No one else around here does either!" the man shouted back angrily.

"Okay," Susan replied. She looked at her accuser. Their eyes met briefly. Again, the anger blazing forth from deep within him overwhelmed her. For a moment, her fear returned so intensely that she could not breathe. Why? What was it about *this* man that would trigger such overwhelming anxiety within her? Then she recognized his face. She *remembered* him. He was one of her accusers from that long ago lifetime, that lifetime when others had so harshly judged her for speaking her truth—judged her...and then *killed* her.

She was sure the man himself remembered nothing of that past life. In fact, she had the strangest feeling that he wasn't angry at *her*, and that she was simply the *target* of his anger. If that was true, and she was sure it was, then none of this was *personal*.

Personal or not, though, her gut-wrenching fear was real...and it had been stimulated in her for a reason.

What reason?

Didn't people draw to themselves the very things they most feared? Yes, but how did that apply in *this* case? What was she most afraid of? This man? No, he was simply playing out a part in her drama. Was she afraid of being hurt? That was closer, but the understanding still eluded her.

Mentally, she summed up what she knew: She was afraid of speaking her truth and then being hurt. *But* she could not be hurt unless she *allowed* it. That meant what she was really afraid of was...what? The understanding she so desperately wanted seemed almost within her grasp. Then the veil dropped, and the understanding disappeared.

In her frustration, she appealed for help. "Oh please, please, don't let me lose this understanding. I want to get this. Please, don't let me lose it."

Susan felt Saint Germain's comforting presence. It was almost as if he was standing beside her, talking to her. Was he? She went within, quieted her mind and her fear, and asked, "Saint Germain, are you there?" Again, she felt his loving presence...but no words. Maybe if she went deeper...

"Hon? Hon?" Jeff was tapping her on the arm.

Jeff's voice startled her. "What? Oh, sorry, I must have been daydreaming," she said.

"Sure...well, it's been a long meeting. Here's your sign-up sheet."

Susan took the notebook and opened it. Half way down the list of names, hastily scrawled in a red felt tip pen, were the words: "Go home traitor!" Was this from the angry man? Or someone else? A small knot of fear formed in her stomach. She took a deep breath, let it out slowly, and reminded herself: "I am the Light and I am safe."

Down on the floor of the gymnasium, an exhausted Mayor Morrisey was finishing up. "I can see we're not all in agreement here tonight. That's fine...I guess. At least it's the American way," he said, not sounding entirely convinced of the rightness of this. "But, you people who haven't taken the card, for god sakes consider the future of this city...consider what it will mean to have our beautiful Mount Shasta occupied by federal troops. Because that's exactly what's going to happen unless you guys change your minds." Having said this, he switched off the microphone.

It was a mostly quiet, subdued crowd that began filing out of the gymnasium.

Susan said good-bye to Evelyn and Veda, promising to call them when she had a meeting time set up. Then she and Jeff left for home.

Chapter Twenty-Six
Repercussions

From *Endtimes*: "The issuing of the debit card was a crisis point—a turning point—for many in the United States.

The issuing of the debit card ushered in another act in the Divine Drama.

It triggered many emotions.

It gave birth to many new destiny paths.

It transformed everyone it touched... and it touched virtually *everyone*."

Sleep eluded Susan that night. At four in the morning, unable to sleep and replaying the events of the town meeting for what seemed like the hundredth time, she was startled by a loud, crashing noise from outside. From the floor next to her bed, Sam lifted his shaggy head, growling softly.

"What is it, Sam?"

At the sound of his name, Sam wagged his bushy tail. He picked up his ears, growled again, sighed, then rested his head on his paw.

Probably some animal checking out our garbage can, she thought to herself. Reaching down, she petted Sam, then left her hand on his warm coat. He thumped his tail on the floor in appreciation.

She looked at her sleeping husband and smiled. Jeff could sleep through *anything*. She turned over, put her head close to his, listened to his rhythmic breathing. Suddenly, her heart filled with love for this man who was her husband. He had grown so much since their move to Mount Shasta, had opened to receive the truth of himself. She was proud of him.

She sighed. Turning onto her back, she closed her eyes and tried to put all thoughts out of her head. But after another 5 minutes of restless tossing, she admitted to herself that she would not sleep for awhile. She got up and found her copy of *Mylokos of Lemuria*. She had read a few chapters in the past weeks, and she had begun to feel a deep connection to this beautiful, ancient land called Lemuria. Opening the book, she read:

> "In the time in which I live, we do not pressure our children to choose a life-path, and many of the inhabitants of my village have no recognizable trade or occupation for many years.
>
> This is difficult to explain. The idea of work as you know it is foreign to our civilization. There are things that need to be done of course: We must gather food and prepare it; we must construct our dwellings; we must fashion our clothing. All of that. But we do this in a different way. We have no separate class of workers such as you have. Those who choose to work choose *freely*; and the choosing is an expression of the love we have for ourselves and for one another.
>
> This would be a difficult idea for most in your society to comprehend, for in *your* time there is much fear surrounding the issue of work. You are taught that you *must* work if you are to live. There is no such fear in our society. There is much abundance and no

fear of survival, for we live in the understanding that the Universe supports us re-
gardless of the path we choose."

Susan put the book down. She sighed. She leaned her
head back on the chair and closed her eyes. How she
yearned to live in a society such as Mylokos described! All
her life she had wanted this! But where was there such a
place? She felt sadness at the thought that no such
community seemed to exist on the Planet at this time. Well,
then, they would have to create one. She didn't know who
the "they" were, or how "they" would create such a
magical kingdom; and at that moment she did not care, for
she was secure in the understanding that if she desired this
deep within her being, and if Spirit wanted this for her, it
was *done*.
    Knowing this brought a great peace to her heart. She
crawled back into bed and was asleep instantly.

She woke the next morning to the sun streaming in
through her bedroom curtains. Suddenly feeling an overwhelming gratitude for the many gifts in her life, her heart
filled with joy.
    Opening the curtains, she greeted the Mountain:

> "Thank you, Mountain, for being here.
> And thank you, Mother Earth,
> for making this Mountain
> and for sharing it with me."

She smiled as she thought of more to be grateful for:

> "Thank you, Saint Germain,
> for being my friend.
> And thank *you*, Susan Langley,
> for being you."

The sound of her own name, spoken aloud, sounded
strange, almost as if it no longer belonged to her.
    After her morning meditations, she went into the
kitchen and sat down at the table with three of her favorite

cookbooks. She had recently visited the local farmer's market, had come away with piles of fresh vegetables, and she wanted some new ways to prepare them.

From the garage came the familiar, comforting sounds of Jeff's puttering. She smiled, opened the first book, and browsed through a recipe for mushroom soup.

"Damn it!" Jeff yelled.

Startled, Susan hurried to the door and peered outside.

Jeff was standing by their car, looking grim. "Better come out here," he said.

"What is it?"

"All the crazies are out," he replied cryptically.

Susan walked down the porch steps and saw what was upsetting Jeff. On the side of the car spray painted in bright red letters was the word, WITCH! Jeff pointed to the house. Turning around, she saw the same word on the front door.

She went to the car, knelt down, and put her hand over the dried paint to read the energy of whoever had done the painting.

Looking worried, Jeff said, "I think we'd better call the sheriff."

Susan shook her head. "Let's wait. They didn't mean any harm. They're upset and they're afraid."

Jeff regarded the foot high letters on the car. "They don't mean any harm? How do you know?"

Susan couldn't explain her ability to read people's energy. She didn't understand exactly what happened or how it happened, only that on some deep, inner level she received information—amazingly accurate information—from *somewhere*. Over the past few months, she had learned to trust the understandings that came to her in this way. "I just know," she said softly.

"You sure?"

"Yes."

Jeff had also learned to trust her intuitions. He relaxed. "They sure made a mess of the car," he sighed.

"Oh well, we were going to get it painted anyway. Right?"

Jeff didn't answer.

Susan laughed. "Or maybe we'll leave it the way it is. It'll be like one of those cars you see with the advertising on the side."

Jeff raised his eyebrows. Sometimes he didn't understand her sense of humor. "It doesn't bother you?" he asked.

"No. At least not in this moment." And it was true—it *didn't* bother her. She knew many people didn't like what she'd said at yesterday's meeting, and they might not like things she would have to say in the future; but she felt none of the gut-wrenching fear that had paralyzed her even a few short days ago. She was challenging people's beliefs, that's all...and some of them didn't like it. But most important, she now understood that *she could do this and not bring injury to herself as she had in that long ago lifetime.*

Looking again at the hastily painted words on the car and on the house, she went inside herself and asked for the truth...for she wanted to be sure she understood; and the understanding she received confirmed her first intuition: She and Jeff were in no danger.

However, her inner voice told her to pay attention to something. True, there was no danger, but these angrily painted words told her *something.* Ah, of course, she was judging herself for speaking out at the meeting; and these crudely painted words were her *mirror*—indeed, *they were her own self judgment mirrored back to her.* No problem, she would ask for clarity and understanding about her self judgment...and then she would heal it. And when she had healed it, she would no longer draw this mirror into her life—she would not *need* to.

Jeff regarded her somewhat skeptically. "I'm glad this doesn't upset you, but just the same I think I'll get the paint off."

Jeff was coming out of the garage with solvent and rags when Vicki and Glenn drove up.

"Painting the car are you?" Glenn joked, motioning to the freshly painted word on the car door.

"Right," Jeff replied, a trace of sarcasm in his voice. "Here, make yourself useful," he said, tossing Glenn one of the rags. "You start on one end, and I'll start on the other."

Glenn took the rag and asked, "So, what's this all about?"

"We attended a town meeting last night to talk about the debit card and the possible takeover of the town by the federal authorities. Have you heard about that?"

"Sure."

"Anyway, people got pretty steamed up. Susan said a few things that pissed off some folks. I think that's what this is about."

Glenn grunted. "I'll tell you, though, this is *nothing* compared to what's happening in the good old Bay Area. Everyone is getting really weirded out down there. That's why we've decided to get out. We're moving up here."

Jeff put down his rag. "Hey great. Glad to hear it Susan will be happy, too."

"Is she okay," Vicki asked, her eyes on the car door.

"Oh sure. A little worried maybe, but not much. She's taking it better than I would. Look, this is all the paint that's going to come off right now. I'll get the rest later. Let's go in and tell Susan the good news."

Jeff piled some of his home made biscuits on a plate, spooned out a generous portion of Evelyn's blackberry jam to go with them, then joined the others on the deck.

"I still can't believe the view you guys have," Glenn remarked. "Mountains, mountains everywhere. And you can really *see* them. In the Bay Area, you have to kind of remember what they look like there's so much smog most of the time."

"That's not what's wrong with the Bay Area," Vicki declared angrily.

Glenn nodded and sighed. "Anyway, the house is up for sale. We're getting out. Moving up here," he said to Susan.

Susan glanced at Glenn and then at Vicki. "Wonderful, but I thought you..." Susan stopped in mid sentence and looked at Vicki.

Vicki's eyes had filled with tears. "Damn...I hate to cry."

"What's the matter?" Susan asked.

Glenn took a deep breath. "Things are happening down in the Bay Area...strange things. They're upsetting Vicki."

"You too, buddy," Vicki reminded him. "You don't like it, either."

"That's true, I don't," Glenn admitted. "I'm beginning to hate the place, too," he added, the anger obvious in his voice.

"Must be really bad," Jeff said.

"It is," Glenn replied. "People have changed since the quake. Turned mean and nasty. Nobody has any patience anymore."

"It's worse than that," Vicki corrected him.

"Yeah, you're right," Glenn acknowledged. "Anyhow, something happened yesterday that pretty much convinced us it's time to go." He shook his head. "God, I still can't believe this happened, but it did. Vicki went shopping at the mall, and she was about to pull into a parking space...I mean there were *lots* of empty spaces, for Chrissake...but this guy got pissed. I guess he figured he got there first."

"No way!" Vicki replied emphatically.

"Anyway, he got pissed and rammed his car into hers. Then he backed up and did it again."

Jeff shook his head in disbelief. "Holy shit, you mean he just deliberately ran into her?"

"Yeah. Didn't hurt Vicki, but sure did a number on the car." Glenn drummed his fingers on the table. "After he hit her the second time, he backed up and took off. Cops never did get him."

"That's weird."

"That kind of stuff is happening all the time now. People are cracking up. Coming unglued."

"I won't live there anymore," Vicki stated. "I don't care if we *do* have to give the house away. That's *it* for me."

"Anyhow, that's the story," Glenn said softly.

"We're seeing some of that crazy energy up here," Susan said.

"Jeff told us about your meeting last night. And we saw what they did to *your* car. You okay?" Vicki asked.

Susan smiled. "Actually, I am. People up here are a little different. They're upset at what's happening, and they're confused, but they aren't quite...they aren't pushed to the edge like they are in the cities."

Vicki fought to hold back her tears. "What *is* happening? People are so *different*. I don't like it. It's like all of a sudden their dark sides have come out. Know what I mean?"

"Sure," Susan answered. "I think it's because events are moving too fast for most people. They feel like their lives are out of control. They're scared. And deep inside, they realize there's more to come—more changes—and they don't understand what to do. You could call it overload. It brings out the angry, scared child."

"*Is* there more to come?" Vicki asked, her voice trembling with fear.

Susan pulled her chair over to where Vicki was sitting. Taking Vicki's hand in her own, she replied, "It feels like it. But we'll be fine... although it helps if you *believe* that. Do you?"

"I think so. But I'll feel even *better* once we get up here."

Squeezing Vicki's hand, Susan said, "I think its a good idea that you're moving. We'll help you guys find a house."

They talked for awhile, until it got too cold to sit on the deck; then they went inside, made a fire, and talked some more. It seemed safe and cozy and warm by the fire...as if someone had turned the clock back to a simpler time when everything at least *appeared* to be normal.

Chapter Twenty-Seven
Susan is Tested

From *Endtimes*: "Those whose dream it was to control the Earth could sense a force beginning to oppose them. They could feel their well thought-out plans beginning to crumble, and they acted swiftly to squash this growing opposition."

It was 10 AM, two days after the town meeting. Vicki and Glenn had just signed a lease on a house a mile farther up on Old Stage Road, and they had dropped by Susan and Jeff's to celebrate. The four of them were sitting around the kitchen table, eating blueberry muffins from the Sunshine Cafe, when a loud and insistent knock rattled the front door. Sam lifted his head and growled menacingly.

"I'll get it," Jeff said. He opened the door to find two large men, in blue suits and red ties, standing on the front porch. His first thought was that they were members of some religious sect wanting to talk to him about the salvation of his soul. On second glance, he concluded that they were not religious types at all. In fact, they had a decidedly hard look to them.

"Yes?" Jeff asked warily.

The taller of the two, a heavyset man with cold gray

eyes, leaned slightly forward and asked, "We are looking for Mrs. Langley. Is this her residence?"

For some reason Jeff did not understand, he was immediately on his guard—and feeling very protective of Susan. "What do you want?" he demanded to know.

The heavyset man repeated his question—only this time his voice had a slight trace of irritation. "We are looking for Mrs. Langley, sir. Is she here?"

"I'm Mrs. Langley," Susan called from the kitchen.

Ignoring Jeff, the heavyset man asked," Mrs. Langley, may we have a few moments of your time?"

"Who *are* you?" Jeff asked.

"We are here to see Mrs. Langley, sir."

"Not until you identify yourselves."

Neither of the men made a move. Then the heavyset man said, "We will identify ourselves to Mrs. Langley if she wishes."

In the meantime, Susan had walked up beside Jeff. "Yes, I *do* want to know who you are."

The heavyset man reached inside his suit and pulled out his wallet. Jeff noticed that he carried a gun in a shoulder holster. The man opened his wallet, flashing his identification. "I am special agent Randolph of the Federal Bureau of Investigation."

The other man, shorter and with a pockmarked face, waited until Randolph had finished. "And I am agent Moses of the World Abundance Corporation."

This surprised Jeff. "The Corporation? You mean the same group in charge of the debit card?"

"That's right, sir," agent Moses replied. "Now, if you don't mind, we would like to speak to Mrs. Langley."

Jeff put himself between Susan and the two agents. "I'm her husband. If there's anything you want to say, you'll have to say it with me present."

"Is that your wish, Mrs. Langley?" agent Randolph asked.

"Yes," Susan replied. "Look, let's go inside and sit down...and then you can ask me what you want."

Jeff squeezed Susan's arm reassuringly. "Sweetie, you

really don't *have* to talk with these guys you know," he said.

"No, it's okay, I want to."

Reluctantly, Jeff moved aside and let the two agents enter. From where he was lying near the table, Sam growled and bared his teeth.

"Easy boy," Jeff urged. But Sam's growl got deeper. "Maybe I'd better put him out. What do you think?" he asked Susan.

"Here, I'll do it," Vicki volunteered. She got up and called Sam: "Come on boy!" But Sam's eyes were fixed on the two agents and he ignored her.

With a glance at Sam, Susan said, "No, wait, he's okay. He'll sit next to me, and then he'll quiet down." As she predicted, Sam sat at her feet; but his eyes never left the two blue-suited strangers.

"These are two friends from the Bay Area," Jeff said, motioning to Vicki and Glenn. The special agents gave them a cursory, almost bored glance, then turned their attention to Susan.

In an attempt to quiet her own nervousness, Susan asked, "Would you like something to drink...some water or something?"

Agent Randolph shook his head no. He reached inside his suit and pulled out a small, well-worn notebook. Flipping it open, he stated, "Mrs. Langley, it has come to our attention that you were at the Mount Shasta town meeting two nights ago. Is that correct?"

"Along with about 500 other people," Jeff was quick to add. "Now, what's this about?"

Ignoring Jeff's remark, agent Randolph continued, "Is that correct, Mrs. Langley?"

"Yes."

"Now, Mrs. Langley, during the course of this meeting did you make a statement to the effect that it was not wise to accept the debit card?"

Susan nodded her head.

"Mrs. Langley, for the record, is that a "yes"?" agent Moses wanted to know.

"It's a yes," Susan answered calmly.

Agent Randolph leaned his head slightly forward and asked, "Specifically, you stated that it was a lie and a trick. Is that correct?"

Susan thought for a moment. "No, what I said *specifically* was that it was a trick and that I had better things to do than to be tricked. But, now that you mention it, I would agree, it's also a lie."

Vicki clapped her hand over her mouth, barely suppressing a giggle.

Agent Randolph raised his eyebrows, "A lie and a trick, Mrs. Langley?"

"Precisely."

Agent Randolph put down his notebook, resting his hands on the table. "Mrs. Langley, I am sure you are aware of the grave crisis facing this country, are you not?"

The man's eyes almost mesmerized Susan. They were not just cold—they were strangely almost reptilian. Susan wondered if he ever blinked. She felt herself being hypnotized, and she shook her head imperceptibly to break the spell. "I realize there are some problems, but I don't see what the country's troubles have to do with what I said or didn't say at the meeting."

Agent Randolph continued to stare.

Susan felt a moment of intense panic, almost as if some unseen force was pulling her into the darkness—no, into the *void*. She pictured herself being pulled under the cold, dark water by a crocodile. She called on the White Light to surround and protect her, and the fear passed through her. She met agent Randolph's intense stare, and she saw a flicker of disappointment in his eyes—the look the hunter might have when it realizes that its prey has escaped. "I was voicing my opinion, and I will continue to do so. I wish no harm to anyone, but, on the other hand, I have no intention of giving away my power...to anyone," she declared calmly, but firmly.

Agent Moses of the Corporation resumed the interrogation, "Mrs. Langley, you must be aware that the government and the Corporation are doing everything they can to get this great country back on its feet. You must also be aware that the debit card is an important element in this recovery."

"It's a damn stupid idea!" Glenn exclaimed.

"It's the law of the land," agent Moses countered, "and we must begin to have more compliance."

"You mean the law says that everyone *has* to take the card?" Jeff asked. "I hadn't heard that."

"It's the will of the country," agent Randolph declared, correcting his partner, but evading Jeff's question. "Do you believe in the will of the people, Mr. Langley?"

"But it isn't actually the *law*."

"It soon will be, I assure you," agent Moses stated, sounding very sure of himself.

"It's not the law yet. There's nothing they can do," Jeff said to Susan.

Agent Randolph held up his hands. "Now, wait a minute, we aren't here to *arrest* you. We're here to enlist your support to help this great country." He paused, a smile, a very *thin* smile, on his face. "Are you a patriot, Mrs. Langley?"

Susan ignored his question. "Why do you care what I think or what I do?"

Agent Randolph took a breath and let it out slowly, all the while measuring Susan with his cold eyes. "Because you are a respected member of this community. People listen to you. And, you have an influential job."

"*My* job is influential? I illustrate children's books."

"We know that," agent Moses answered smugly. "You work for the Allison Book Company. The Allison Book Company publishes books for children between four and eight years of age. The Allison Book Company publishes fiction with a humanistic slant." He spat out these facts with an almost robotic precision. "So you see, Mrs. Langley, you reach many children in your work. What could be more influential than that?"

Susan was beginning to catch on. She smiled. "You think I'm going to turn the children of America against the government and against the Corporation. Right?"

Agent Moses shrugged his shoulders. "It's been done before. Perhaps it would not be a conscious decision on your part. But it's your attitude that counts, Mrs. Langley. Your attitude would come out in your work, and right now we believe your attitude to be very, very negative...and very un-American."

Susan was starting to enjoy this sparring. "Mm, I see. So, if I don't go along, if I don't agree to an attitude change, then what? Are you going to get me fired?"

Agent Randolph shook his head. "Oh, I don't think anything as extreme as that is called for. That would be carrying things too far, don't you think?"

Susan didn't answer. She stared at agent Randolph, and for an instant his eyes registered his discomfort. Then he regained his composure, and the look left his eyes.

Agent Moses took over. "We simply want you to be a good team player and to rethink your position on the card."

"I don't have to rethink it. I've already decided I'm not going to take it. What others do is their business, but I'm clear that I'm not taking the debit card." Susan leaned forward until her face was only inches away from agent Randolph. She was so close she could smell the cloying aroma of his after-shave, a brand she had always disliked. "You see, the thing is, I've never been a good team player. Team player is one of those code words, know what I mean? Like calling a certain section of a city a "high crime area" when what you really mean is that it's mostly Black. Well, team player is like that. It's a code word, at least the way *you* are using it. And you know what it's a code word for?"

Neither agent answered and neither agent blinked.

"What it really means is *compromise*. Good team players are people who are willing to give up their identity in order to fit in. They are people who are willing to compromise their beliefs for the good of the team. No thanks."

"I see," agent Moses said. "So, we can't get you to change your mind? Or at least to think about it?"

"Nope."

"Very well, then, we are finished with you," agent Randolph stated.

"Are you going to talk to other people who were at the meeting?" Susan asked... although she knew they were intending to do just that.

Agent Randolph smiled his thin smile. "We might. Good day, Mrs. Langley."

"Holy shit!" Glenn exclaimed, after the two agents had left. "Where'd they dig up *those* two?"

"I'm going to lose my job," Susan said calmly. "Somehow they're going to persuade Allison to fire me. It's their way of punishing me for not going along with their schemes. And they hope the word will get around and that others will think twice before refusing the card. Not very creative, but it may scare some people."

"Look, I have a good lawyer friend. I bet she could help," Glenn offered.

"No, everything's okay. I think it's time for me to be doing something else with my life, so everything's working out fine."

"You sure? It wouldn't be any problem to call her. She'd *love* something like this."

"I'm sure."

"I think you should at least talk to her," Jeff suggested. He sounded worried.

"No, I'm fine."

Jeff threw his hands up in the air. "Okay."

Susan realized that the visit by the two agents meant something different to her than it did to Jeff or Glenn or Vicki. For them, it had been a cause of fear and worry. For her, though, the visit was a gift from Spirit. It had opened a doorway. She had stepped though the doorway, and she now stood firmly on her path. She knew what Spirit wanted her to do—and her heart opened in joy at the thought of following her Spirit.

She silently sent her love and her support to the others on the agent's list, hoping they were open to receiving a similar gift.

Chapter Twenty-Eight
Friends Gather Again

> Revelations: 22:1: And he showed me a
> pure river of water of life, clear as crys-
> tal, proceeding out of the throne of God
> and of the Lamb.

The Divine Drama unfolded rapidly in the next few days.

Mount Shastans continued to balk at the pressure being exerted on them to take the debit card, and their acceptance rate inched up a scant 2 percent, from 33 percent to 35 percent.

True to their word, the Corporation, acting under the authority of the Debit Card Law, sent in their own personnel to govern Mount Shasta. Two members of an elite FEMA unit specially trained by the Corporation replaced the city council, and federal troops replaced the eight person police force. The Corporation stationed other federal troops at the town armory. These troops occasionally patrolled the town's streets.

The little mountain town was now literally in the Corporation's hands. It was an "occupied territory."

Similar takeovers occurred in many other areas. All together, the Corporation seized more than eighteen hundred cities and towns across the United States. In some areas, they occupied whole counties. The media downplayed these takeovers, claiming that they were an isolated occurrence, and that except for a few isolated rural areas, most Americans had gladly accepted the card.

This was not the truth.

As soon as the Corporation had seized control of Mount Shasta, they began exerting tremendous pressure on local businesses to comply with the new Debit Card Law. Most establishments succumbed. A few did not. Among the holdouts was the Sunshine Cafe.

The Corporation increased the pressure on this popular Mount Shasta business. Visits by the health inspector became a daily and annoying occurrence; and the city building inspector suddenly insisted that an outdoor patio opened a few months ago was not in compliance with the city building codes.

The cafe weathered these bureaucratic assaults.

The cafe itself became a symbol of resistance. Many in Mount Shasta vowed to keep it open no matter what, and business boomed as more and more residents flocked to the popular Mount Shasta restaurant to demonstrate their anti-Corporation sentiments. Susan and Jeff were awed by the number of patrons who squeezed themselves into the cramped quarters of the tiny cafe.

The most serious pressure came from the Bank of the Western United States, the bank that had loaned the cafe the money to complete their recent renovations. Citing an obscure technicality, the bank informed them that they were calling in the loan. The cafe had two weeks to come up with five thousand dollars. On top of this bad news, the next day's mail brought a certified letter from the absentee landlord telling them of his decision not to renew their lease. The cafe vowed to fight these pressures, although Susan and Jeff and others secretly doubted how long they could hold out.

Meanwhile, Susan's own unusual odyssey continued to unfold.

As she predicted, she lost her job. One week after the visit by the two special agents, she received a letter from her publishing company informing her that, due to an unexpected downturn in the children's book publishing business, they were, regrettably, terminating her contract. Susan knew this was not the *real* reason for her dismissal.

Over the next few days, she learned that special agents Randolph and Moses had indeed visited other Mount Shasta residents. They had "dropped in" on Nancy the photographer and the man who had supported Susan at the meeting. Also "interviewed" were Anna and Veda and the others who had put their names on Susan's sign-up sheet.

Two weeks after her own interview, acting on prompting from her inner guidance, Susan began calling people on the list. Her guidance told her that it was time for them to gather together, to share their energy and their love.

She began with the thirty-two names on the sign-up sheet. Of these, she reached twenty four people. Three declined to be involved. Reading their energy on the phone, Susan sensed their fear. She understood it, didn't judge it, and silently wished them well.

That left twenty-one people.

Several were quite eager to meet—others were in various states of indecision.

Susan invited all interested parties to get together at her house in two day's time.

By 7:30, fourteen people had gathered in Susan's living room: Jeff and herself, Vicki and Glenn, and ten who had signed up at the town meeting, including four from the channeling group.

Even though many people were smiling or laughing, the energy in the room was intense. Susan was nervous as she began speaking. "I'm happy to see you again. I feel there's a great purpose to us being here tonight. Does anyone else feel this?"

"Yes!" Anna exclaimed joyfully. "I feel it! There's wonderful energy in this room tonight!"

Evelyn nodded in agreement. "There *is* a purpose work-

ing here. Many of you have been in my dreams. I knew
we'd be connecting in some physical way soon."

"I had a dream like that, too," Karen added.

Several people, including Susan, nodded, as if they had
dreamed similar dreams.

Anna looked around the room and asked, "Did everyone get a glass of water? The vibrations are pretty intense
in here, so it's a good idea to drink lots of water."

Several people took Anna's advice. Susan waited until
everyone had settled down. She wanted to say something to
get the group more focused, but she followed an even
stronger prompting to be quiet and simply allow things to
unfold.

"So, what do you think about the troops in town?" a
red-haired woman of about forty asked. Like most people
in Mount Shasta, she looked vaguely familiar to Susan.

"Reminds me of Berkeley in the 60's," a bearded man
on Susan's left replied.

The woman sitting next to Susan leaned around her and
asked him, "Were you in Berkeley in the 60's?"

"Yeah, were you there, too?"

"Sure. I was finishing up at Cal. Well, I'll be darned.
Small world, as they say. My name's Kate."

"Hi Kate, I'm Jerry," the bearded man responded. Then
he looked at each of them. "Some of you I know and some
I don't. Maybe we could start off by introducing ourselves.
My name is Jerry. Oh, I guess I already said that."

"Which way are we going?" Veda asked, laughing nervously.

"Why not start your way," Jerry suggested.

"Okay, I'm Veda."

"My name is Anna."

"I'm Jeff, and this scruffy dog is Sam."

"Glenn."

"Vicki."

"I'm Andrew."

"Oh, is it my turn. I'm not very good at these
things...but, anyway, my name is Brian."

"Nancy Macintosh."

"Nancy, did you bring any of your photos?" Susan asked.

"Yes, I brought a few to share."

"Great. Maybe you could pass them around after the meeting."

"Sure."

"Want me to say my name?" the red-haired woman asked impatiently.

"Sure," Susan said. "Sorry."

"I'm Connie."

"Karen."

"My name is Evelyn. I must tell you about Emil and Cassandra. They can't be here tonight, but they love this idea, and they will attend the next meeting."

Kate waited for Evelyn to finish. "I'm Kate."

"Susan."

With the introductions over, no one knew what to say, until Jeff asked, "So, Jerry, why were those troops in Berkeley?"

"It was during the People's Park thing. Remember that?"

"No."

"Well, maybe I'll tell you about it sometime. Anyway, I remember I was living a few blocks from the campus, on one of those little Berkeley side streets, and I woke up one morning...and there was this tank parked outside my bedroom window. Pretty freaky."

"What happened?"

"They weren't there too long. Guess the powers that be decided we weren't a danger to overthrow the government, so one day the troops up and pulled out."

"Wish they'd pull out of Mount Shasta," Kate began, "but it sure feels like they're here to stay. At least there aren't any tanks."

Andrew held up his hand. "Remember me?" he asked Susan.

"Sure, Andrew. Glad you could come. How's your dog?"

"She's doing fine. She's up on the Mountain at my

campsite," Andrew replied in his slow and deliberate style. "What I wanted to say to this lady here," he went on, turning to face Kate, "is that they got tanks down the road, down in Redding. Reason I know is, I was down there yesterday pasting some of my flyers around town, and I saw them. There's more than a hundred, I reckon. They've got them parked in a big deserted lot. Built a wire fence around them. I'm not saying this to upset you. Thought you'd like to know is all."

Kate nodded but said nothing.

Jerry looked worried. "Are there tanks in the streets?"

"None that I could see," Andrew replied.

Susan felt the tension in the room, and the rising fear, and she wanted to shift the energy if she could. "I'd really like to talk about *us*. Do you think we could do that?"

"I agree," Evelyn added, flashing her beautiful smile. "Heck, we're just creating a bad scenario for ourselves with this talk about tanks and troops. That's someone else's drama. It sure isn't mine. No offense to those of you who appear to be interested in tanks."

"None taken," Jerry responded quickly. "I agree with you."

Veda leaned forward in her chair. She spoke so softly most in the room had to strain to hear. "It's important to remember the beauty and the power that we are. The Masters wanted me to remind you of that. I also want to let you know that Saint Germain has offered to channel some of his thoughts about what is taking place, tomorrow night at Evelyn's."

Susan had been hoping for this. "Great. He's going to get lots of questions."

Veda smiled shyly. "He knows that and he's ready."

"Now," Susan continued, "as I'm sure you're aware, there's lots going on, and even though it can be kind of exciting, it can also be stressful. So I'm being prompted to find out if anyone in the group needs assistance."

Kate raised her hand. "We do. My husband Ted didn't come tonight. He's mad at me for being involved in this group. You see, what happened is that right after the town

meeting—after I signed up for *this* meeting—right after
that Ted couldn't get any work. He's a carpenter, and all of
a sudden there's no work. He says it's because we didn't
take the debit card...and because I signed up for this
meeting. I guess some folks in town think we're subver-
sive. So, they won't hire Ted as long as I'm in this group.
Anyway, we're running out of money and we can't pay our
rent and..." She stopped and the tears rolled down her
cheeks. "We may have to move back to Oregon to live with
my parents. I hate to think of leaving, but..."

"I think maybe I can help," Brian said. "I have a large
house. There's a cottage out back. Hasn't been used in
years, so it needs some cleaning, and the porch railing kind
of sags, but...how many in your family?"

"Just Ted and myself."

"Oh, great, it would be perfect for two people. You're
welcome to use it if you need to. And don't worry about
rent."

"It wouldn't be an imposition?"

"No, not at all. I'd be glad for the company. I *need*
some company. At least I *think* I do. People tell me I keep
too much to myself."

"Need any kind of carpentry work done? I'm sure Ted
would be glad to trade for rent."

"Maybe. We can talk about it. But don't worry about
it."

Anna was next. "We have extra food for anyone who
needs it. Evelyn and I planted an absolutely *huge* garden.
Didn't we?" she asked Evelyn. She put a large arm around
Evelyn, drawing her close, almost jerking the tiny woman
out of her chair.

"Yep, and I have the blisters to prove it," Evelyn added.
"Anna's right, we have tons of veggies. More than we can
use."

"Hm, what a *coincidence*," Susan said, a knowing smile
on her face. "Jeff and I want to plant a garden, but with
everything that's happening it never seems to get done.
You need any help weeding or watering or something like
that?"

Evelyn and Anna looked at each other and burst out laughing. Then Anna said, "Funny you should mention that, we were just talking about making the garden more of a community project. We'd love to have you involved. So, anyone who wants to come by and weed or water or just sit and bless the plants, we'd love it."

Connie raised her hand. "I'd be interested in that."

"So would I," Jerry added.

"Me too," Vicki said. "I've never done much gardening, but I'd like to learn."

Evelyn smiled. "Glad to have you all."

After a moment of silence, Nancy said, "This feels like a family to me. It's almost like we've known each other before, and now we're renewing our friendships. How do the rest of you feel?"

"That's exactly how it is," Veda affirmed. "I'm having the same understanding. It's wonderful."

"It sure is," Nancy added. "I've been staying here with friends. I always figured I'd be moving on—maybe to Colorado—but now I think I'll stay. I don't know about you, but I *need* a group like this. I need *you* guys. I don't want to go through this all by myself. I want people I can share my life with. I'm staying."

Several people clapped. Kate, who was sitting next to Nancy, put her arm around her.

"Oh, and Nancy, if you need a place to live, I have an extra bedroom," Connie volunteered. "Only thing is, I live out of town a bit. Quite a bit actually. Up by the old dairy."

"Oh, I *love* that area!" Nancy exclaimed happily. "The light out there is great for taking photographs."

"Wonderful. Hope you don't mind sharing the house with two inquisitive cats."

"Nope, I love cats."

Jerry was next. "This may sound like a pretty far-out idea, and it's probably not real practical, but I just got this hit that one of these days we may be living together. I don't mean in one house, but maybe in a little community. I lived in a commune for awhile in the 60's, but…it didn't work out. I've always wanted to try it again. Maybe this is the time. Not right away of course, but..." His voice trailed off into uncertainty.

"Hm, this is interesting," Glenn said. "I've never been a big fan of group living, but, sitting here listening to you, I have the strangest feeling it's going to happen. And the *really* strange thing is, I can see myself being involved. Never thought I'd say *that*."

Jeff looked at Jerry and asked, "You mean a smaller community than we have in Mount Shasta, right?"

"Yeah," Jerry answered tentatively. "Maybe like a couple of hundred acres...with a few cabins or little houses. Like, room enough so that nobody's squished together. Then maybe a central building for meetings and potlucks. Something like that."

"Sounds wonderful, folks," Evelyn chimed in. "But you know me, I'm very practical. How would we pay for it?"

It was Andrew's turn. "It's like when I needed money for me and my dog, and you two kind people helped me out," he said to Susan and Jeff. "It would happen like that. As long as we asked for the God Force to be with us, we'd have enough."

"Andrew's right, I've seen lots of other things happen that way," Nancy affirmed.

Connie's face registered her doubt. "No, no, now wait! Even if we had the money, how would we buy the land? Or pay our taxes?"

Susan frowned. "I don't understand."

"Who in this group has a debit card?" Connie asked. When no one raised their hand, she continued, "See, that's what I mean. Everything has to be done with the card...but nobody *has* one."

"Jeff and I would be willing to contribute some of our gold or silver towards this project."

"I would, too," Evelyn added. "And there are others."

Connie shook her head. "That's fine...but how long do you think the Corporation is going to let people get away with using gold or silver? Not long I bet."

Susan sighed. "You might be right...except I know that we can find a way. I *know* it."

Connie shrugged her shoulders and did not reply.

"Who would run the place?" Karen asked.

At first no one had an answer. Then Brian suggested, "Perhaps we'd *all* run it."

Kate looked skeptical. "I don't mean to be contrary, but don't you have to have just one or two people running something like that?"

Susan was impulsed to speak. "Let's hold this dream in our hearts, and let's let it grow there. The answers we're seeking will come from that process...if that's our intention. We have a wonderful start here. Let's get together again soon and let the idea bloom. How about if we meet again after the channeling?" Everyone agreed.

Susan said good-bye to friends old and new. Watching them leave, she had the understanding that they had put something into motion, something wondrous, something that would change their lives forever—and perhaps the lives of others also.

Chapter Twenty-Nine
Community

Revelations: 22:17: And the Spirit and
the bride say, Come. And let him that
heareth say, Come. And let him that is
athirst come. And whosoever will, let
him take the water of life freely.

Although the next channeling was open to anyone who
wanted to attend, the only people to gather in Evelyn's
living room were those who had recently met at Susan's.
As Veda explained it later, "You were the only folks who
needed to come. The others are on a different path, so they
made a decision on some deep level not to attend—it
wasn't really *their* meeting."

As was her custom, Veda led them in a short
meditation. Then Saint Germain began speaking,
"Greetings, beloved ones. It is indeed a grand occasion, this
meeting of ours. How are you this evening?"

A chorus of "Fines!" and "Greats!" greeted Saint Germain's question.

Saint Germain smiled. "How is it that you can be so
wonderful when your whole way of life is falling apart?
And so rapidly I might add."

"That's a good question," someone whispered.

"Indeed, it *is* a good question. Is anyone in the understanding of this?" Saint Germain waited calmly. When it was clear that no one was ready to answer, he continued, "Then I will tell you. It is because deep inside you know there is no loss in this crumbling away of the old, and that indeed even the *idea* of loss is but an illusion."

"Saint Germain," Susan began, "I don't have a question about what you said. I guess there are still times when I get caught up in the illusion of loss, and then I get upset because it feels like something valuable is being destroyed; but I can get myself back to the true understanding pretty quickly these days." She took a deep breath. "There's something else going on, though. There's a certain feeling I'm having, a feeling I think many others here are sharing with me. It's a buoyancy—that's the best way I can describe it. Can you say something about this?"

"Indeed, beloved one. It is precisely this feeling of buoyancy, as you term it, that we will be discussing this evening. It is why you have gathered together on this night. Does anyone wish to speak more on this?"

"Well, I'm not exactly sure what it is, but I have a guess," Jerry volunteered. "I can only talk for myself, but I feel almost removed from what's happening in the outside world these days—like in a way it doesn't concern me—and this gives me a certain kind of inner calmness. That's great, but what's *really* turning me on is that I finally have a *purpose!* Maybe I don't see it yet, but I'm sure it's there, and it feels *wonderful.* My life *finally* has a purpose! It's like when I was a hippie back in the 60's—suddenly life seemed full and exciting and wonderful! Except back then I was *missing* something—I was missing a purpose. It's been a long time, but now I'm about to understand what my purpose is."

"Mm. Indeed, you *do* have a purpose, each of you," Saint Germain said.

"Jerry's right," Kate said. "I'm having the same feeling of purpose. To me it feels like we're *all* involved...all of us in this room. Like we have some kind of group destiny. Can that be true?"

"Indeed. The purpose— *your* purpose —is truly a divine one…and it is *shared*. And the unfoldment of this your purpose brings with it the birthing of a true joy and a true excitement within you—within your *hearts* —that most of you have not known for eons. Is that not wonderful?"

Saint Germain's words touched them deep within their hearts, deep within their soul memories, and many in the room were crying. "Yes, it is wonderful," Anna whispered through her tears. "It's what I've been waiting for my whole life."

"Me too," someone else murmured.

"And it will not be long in coming, you know, for that which is taking place, and which will *continue* to take place, is like unto a dream you have, a dream that has lain buried deep within you—within your *hearts* —these many lifetimes. It is now time to bring this dream into manifestation."

"What *is* this dream?" Jeff asked.

"It is the dream of brotherhood and of sisterhood and of true community," Saint Germain answered. "It is a dream you in this room are committed to bring to fruition, for you are special entities. You are the pioneers and the *way-show-ers*. You will be showing others—indeed, you will be showing *the whole of the world*—how to manifest true love and true harmony in a community. It has been done but seldom upon this your planet you know."

"Are you talking about an actual community? Like we were discussing the other night at Susan's?" Karen wanted to know.

"Precisely, beloved one."

"You mean we're all going to live together?" Vicki asked.

"You may if you wish. There are many ways to create community you know. Perhaps it is that each of you will involve yourselves in the planning of this community, but it may be that not all of you will dwell therein. You would still all be creators, would you not?"

"So it's no accident that we all met at Susan's?" Brian asked. "Or that we're here speaking with you tonight? I mean, it's planned in a way. Perhaps by our higher selves. Like when two people who need to be together for some reason are prompted to be in a certain place at a certain time."

"Indeed, you are in the understanding of this."

It was Nancy's turn to ask a question. "Why *this* particular group of people?"

Saint Germain did not answer.

Connie shifted around in her chair, staring intently at everyone. "I feel like I know all of you from someplace. Does this feeling of familiarity have anything to do with it?"

"Indeed," Saint Germain answered.

Connie did not seem satisfied. "Okay, but I still don't get why *this* particular group?" she asked.

"Because you have been together before in another such community, and you are coming together again to recreate that wondrous experience."

"It's weird, I had that thought tonight, but it seemed too far out," Anna said. "Where was this community?"

Saint Germain took a moment before answering. "You were in Lemuria." Then, after another moment of silence he asked, "Do you remember?"

Anna shook her head no.

Susan took a deep breath. Her eyes filled with tears. "Oh, *I* do. I remember a place, a beautiful place long ago. I see lots of water and lush green vegetation. I see round houses and happy, smiling people. We were smaller and very brown. We lived simply. Is this the time of which you speak?"

Saint Germain smiled. "Precisely. There was much in the way of wisdom that you gained in that lifetime, much that you can now use in this your present undertaking. And you can remember more if you choose." He gazed deeply into Susan's eyes. "Especially you, blessed one. You especially can retrieve these wondrous memories, for you loved your life there dearly, did you not?"

Many emotions flooded Susan's being. She couldn't speak. Saint Germain waited patiently. Finally, she said, "I *was* happy. It's the happiest I've ever been on this planet I think." Then she remembered something else from that lifetime, something she was not quite ready to share with the group.

"Do you think we were all there?" Kate asked.

"Indeed, at one time you all lived within the same *village*. Is that not wondrous?"

"Can we really bring that back?" Connie asked.

"But of course. In truth, that experience has never left the Earth plane. It has, you might say, slipped aside into another dimension; but it has always existed on your planet Earth, so of *course* you may bring it back. You have only to intend it and open your hearts to receive it and it is done."

"Saint Germain, brother," Andrew began, "I know that this project of which you speak is something I want to do. It's my dream like it is these other folks. But why do we undertake this *now?*"

"Because you *need* each other now. You need and you desire the loving *support* of those who are closest to you, those who are your true family, those who may be even closer to you than the ones you call your biological family."

"You mean we here are a family?"

"Is this not your understanding?"

Andrew scratched his head. "I guess it is. I never really had a family, except for my dog. I left home when I was eleven, and I never went back."

"Indeed, it was your path to travel here and there, and a family would have, let us say, kept you in one place. It would have restricted you. Yet now the Universe is bringing you another family, is it not?"

"Yes, and I am grateful. And, brother Germain, I know what you mean about the support. It's getting harder and harder for me to be on my own, traveling around doing the Lord's work. It sure would be nice to have some place to come back to," Andrew said. "Course, I'm not saying I'd stay there permanent. I might get the urge to go and post some of my flyers someplace, but I guess that would be okay, too. I guess I could always come back…if that would be okay with everybody," he asked, glancing shyly at the others.

Glenn raised his hand. "I don't understand, are you saying that we will need each other for emotional support?"

"Precisely."

"Why?"

"There are many whose intent it is to trick you and to confuse you," Saint Germain replied. "You will find it helpful to have others to talk to about such matters. It will be emotionally comforting for you to have these others to share your experiences with," he added. "But there is also much physical cooperation that will soon become necessary. You will find, shortly, that you cannot "go it alone" as you once did. So, it will benefit you to gather into small communities, of perhaps twenty or thirty people, to help each other. This is not so clear now, but in a short time your world will change even more drastically, and many of the services you now take for granted will no longer be available upon your planet."

"Are you talking about things like supermarkets and other kinds of stores?" Glenn asked.

"And other services as well. You will find that you will need to draw on your own resources, and the resources of those close to you, much more than you do now."

Kate asked, "Are there lots of other groups like this one? I mean, is there going to be an explosion of these little communities?"

"Not exactly. Indeed, there *are* others…a *few* others…who are following your path and are coming together for the purpose of true community. But, it is as I have stated, you are the pioneers and the way-showers. You are, let us say, more ready for this grand undertaking than are most others on your planet. They will watch, and they will learn from you…and they will benefit greatly."

Glenn looked skeptical. "Even if you are right, how would we afford something like this? It would take quite a bit of money, for land and houses and the like. Maybe millions. Where would that come from?"

Before Saint Germain could reply, Vicki interjected, "I don't understand much about this, but I do believe that we are provided for, and that if we want this, if we *really* want it, the money will be there."

"Precisely, beloved one."

"But wait, there's something else," Glenn said. "It's something Connie brought up at our last meeting. Look, the law says we can't use gold or silver or barter. I know that lots of people are ignoring the law and getting away with it, but it's my feeling that pretty soon the Corporation is going to clamp down on all this. Then what? How would we buy the land or the supplies we need without a debit card? And even if we could figure a way around all this, what's to prevent the Corporation from sending their goon squad onto our place and just closing it down? My god, they've occupied a thousand or so cities across the country, so coming in and taking us over would be a piece of cake."

It seemed to those in the room that Saint Germain took forever to answer. "Do you not know, beloved one, that there are many in this your country who are not in compliance with the laws of the land? Many who do not pay taxes for instance. And never have."

"Okay...but lots of them get caught. Personally, I don't want to live like an outlaw, always worrying about the Feds catching up with me." Several in the room nodded, as if agreeing with Glenn.

"What is your understanding of the motivation of these you call outlaws?"

"They have mixed motives I'm sure."

"Indeed. Some resist the powers that be for the pleasure of resisting. Others because those they live with expect it of them. But many, many in your country *have simply decided that tyranny is not to be a part of their lives*. They have intended this, and it is so. And they are invisible to those who would control them."

"Invisible?"

"Precisely. They lead simple lives, they call no attention to themselves, and they intend that peace and harmony surround them and protect them, much as a warm blanket protects the wearer against a cold winter wind. And they are invisible. They live, you might almost say, in another dimension."

"I'd like to believe that, but..." Glenn's voice trailed off, and he stared down at the floor.

"Some of the answers you seek may be what you would call slow in coming. And there will be times when your Spirit will call upon you to pursue a course of action without any certainty of the outcome. During these times, you must trust that if you follow your Spirit without hesitation all is well." Saint Germain surveyed the room with his knowing eyes. "I can read your thoughts, beloved ones: many here are saying that this is not much to go on, and that they want for more solid protection...and yet I will say to you again, your only real safety lies in the following of your Spirit. You will see."

"Saint Germain," Kate began, "maybe I'm seeing problems where there are none, but it seems that there's a little more to it than what you've told us. You make it sound so *easy*, like we just have to *want* this and it's done. There has to be more to it than that. Right? Aren't there lots of practical-type details that we would need to consider?"

"It is not as complicated as perhaps you are believing," Saint Germain responded. "Of course, you live in a physical world, so there are practical steps that must be taken—you must obtain the land, and the like. But you have only to intend that these procedures be easy and effortless and joyful, and they will be." Saint Germain paused, as if collecting his thoughts. "There is one more thing that might be of assistance to you. It will help you greatly to put much thought into your overall intentions for this community. You can state these very simply. I am not talking about pages and pages of rules and regulations. You *do* like to have your books of rules and regulations you know—it makes many of you feel safe. But that of which I speak is more of an *intention* or a *purpose* than a compilation of rules. Is this in your understanding?"

Several in the audience shook their heads no.

"All right. Let us say, for example, that you decide that it is your intention that *all who live in your community will honor the sovereignty of all others in your community*. This is an example of what I mean. There are other general principles you may wish to be explicit about. Be brief and be clear."

"Saint Germain, would you talk a little more about some of the practical details of such a community?" Jeff asked.

"It is not my purpose to discuss such matters this evening, for to give you the answers you seek would be to undermine your confidence in your own abilities. You will find much wisdom in each of you. Gather together in groups for the purpose of discussing such issues. Draw upon your *memories* — especially your memories of your shared life in the land you call Lemuria. And of course, I will always be available for further consultation."

"Okay."

"You may be surprised how easy it is, beloved one."

Jeff looked at Saint Germain and nodded.

"There will be other times when we will gather together in groups such as this, for the purpose of a grand sharing of energies and ideas, but for now it is my wish to bid you a fond good evening. Until we meet again, beloved ones."

As Veda was coming out of her trance, Susan looked at these people who were now her family. They had many dreams to dream and much to bring into manifestation, and her heart opened to the joy of this coming experience.

Before she bid her friends goodnight, Susan had one more thing to say. "I want to share something with you. In the past few minutes, I've had some very beautiful visions, of us and of this community we are birthing. I will share this with you the next time we meet...which will be soon." She stopped. "Give me a minute," she said, wiping away her tears. "There's something else. It's about the lifetime in Lemuria. It's all coming back. It's coming back into my memory and into my body. I *remember*. I remember who I was then. I was a woman called Alana. And oh, it was so beautiful in that lifetime, so beautiful and so loving. What I want to say is that Alana has lived within me all this time. She has lived within me all the lifetimes I've had since Lemuria, and *she has waited for this time.* Alana is *me.* She always has been. So, I've decided to take this as my name in *this* lifetime. This is my name now. I am Alana."

Nothing really ever ends,
and so this story is to be
continued in Book Two:
Homecoming.

About the Author

Michael Colin Macpherson

Like Susan, the character in *Remembering*, I too was pulled to MT Shasta...by Spirit.

I live a few miles from the Mountain, with my wife Mary Ann and our three cats, Mr. Squeaks, Miss Mickey and Sasha. I write, I putter in the garden and I occasionally offer my services as a spiritual guide. This keeps my brain busy, so that, hopefully, it does not get in the way of my *real* work...which is to follow Spirit without hesitation.

ORDER FORM

All Prices include tax, shipping and handling*

Remembering $12.00 ea:

Quantity_____$___

Total enclosed$___

*books shipped special fourth class book rate. Please allow 2-3 weeks for delivery. For Air Mail, add $2.00 for 1st book and $.50 for each additional book

Make checks or money orders payable to:

Michael Colin Macpherson

Name

Street address or P.O. Box

City   State   Zip

Phone

checks must be U.S. funds drawn on U.S. bank

Bookstores: please write for discounts

**Green Duck Press
PO Box 651
MT Shasta, CA 96067**